James Albert Frye

From Headquarters

Odd Tales Picked up in the Volunteer Service

James Albert Frye

From Headquarters
Odd Tales Picked up in the Volunteer Service

ISBN/EAN: 9783337080150

Printed in Europe, USA, Canada, Australia, Japan

Cover: Foto ©Andreas Hilbeck / pixelio.de

More available books at **www.hansebooks.com**

FROM HEADQUARTERS

ODD TALES

PICKED UP IN THE VOLUNTEER SERVICE

BY

JAMES ALBERT FRYE

BOSTON

ESTES AND LAURIAT

1893

TO THE

FIRST INFANTRY

M.V.M.

PREFACE.

―∘∘⦂∘⦂∘∘―

IN the odd though truthful tales here
brought together — of which, by the
way, some already have been in print —
there is not the slightest attempt at pen
portraiture, nor is there any pretence to the
accuracy of the military historian; in other
words, this is a collection of chance yarns,
and not a portrait gallery — and no one is
asked to believe that either the Nineteenth
Army Corps or the "Old Regiment" ever
were found in any situations like those in
which they here find themselves placed.

This book, perhaps, may fall into the
hands of one of those — and they are far
too many — whose habit it is to scoff at the
volunteer service, and to look askance at all

who enter it. I sincerely trust that it may, for I wish to say — and in all earnestness — that the militia of today is not the militia of thirty, twenty, or even ten years ago; that nowadays the incompetent and the vicious are allowed to remain in civil life, and are not given places in the ranks of the volunteers; and that those who take the solemn oath of enlistment do so with the full understanding that they will be required to devote their time, their money, and their best energies to the service, and that they have assumed an obligation to fit themselves carefully and intelligently for the duties of a soldier.

The volunteer service of the present time means, to those who find themselves enrolled in it, something more than a mere pastime; and if those who hold it in small esteem could but know of the faithful, conscientious, and untiring work that, from year's end to year's end, is being done in armory and camp, they would leave unsaid, it seems to me, the half-contemptuous words that too often come to the ears of the hard-working, long-suffering, and unrewarded citizen-soldier.

It has been said that the best is none too good for the service of the Commonwealth. If this be true, — and who can question it? — the stigma of whatever blemishes have been found in the militia must be borne by those men of ability and position who, while ever ready to point out weaknesses and faults, negligently have left to hands less competent, or, it may be, less worthy, the work which they themselves were in honor bound to do.

J. A. F.

CONTENTS.

THE PLUCK

OF

CAPTAIN PENDER, C.S.N.

THE PLUCK

OF

CAPTAIN PENDER, C.S.N.

WELL up town, something above quarter of a mile beyond the massive, battlemented armory in which we of the Third Infantry have our headquarters, a side street, branching off from one of the main thoroughfares, ambitiously stretches away until it finds its farther progress barred by a high, stone-capped, brick wall. There it stops. Beyond lie the quadruple tracks of a railway, over which, all day long — and, for that matter, all night, too — thunder the coming and going trains, with such an outpouring of smoke and downpouring of cinders that it is small wonder that a quiet street, such as this one pretends to be, should have lost all desire to continue its course in that direction.

A few paces from the end of the *cul-de-sac*
formed by the halting street and the obstruct-
ing wall, and facing a lamp-post which awk-
wardly rears itself up from the curbstone to
present for inspection a glass panel lettered
"Battery Court," there is — in one of the
long row of houses — an opening which looks
like the entrance to a tunnel.

In point of fact, it *is* the entrance to a
tunnel, for, in order to reach the court
which lies hidden beyond, one has to grope
through fifty feet of brick-bound darkness.
And even when that venture has been
made, the change from shade to light is not
a startling one, for the court is small and entirely surrounded by lofty buildings, so that
one standing in it and looking up at the patch
of blue sky overhead feels much as if he had
landed at the bottom of a well, and instinctively glances about in search of a rope by
which to climb up and out again.

It is an odd corner — and oddly utilized.
All around it stretch streets of dwellings,
but in this silent and dim court the few
structures are plainly and solidly built, and
heavily shuttered with iron, for they all are
devoted to storage.   It was the lack of

breathing space, I dare say, and the close proximity of the railway that made this nook undesirable for any other purpose; and in all probability "Battery Court" would be unknown to-day if we had not happened to stumble upon it in our search for a place where we could pitch our tent, without being forced to pitch after it a king's ransom in the shape of rent.

Facing the dark passageway which offers the only avenue for escape to the street beyond, and entirely filling one end of the court, there looms up a five-storied warehouse. For four stories it bears a perfect family resemblance to its companions on either hand, and up to that height its dull, red bricks and rusty, red iron entitle it to no distinction whatever. But the *fifth* story is altogether another story, and though from an architect's point of view it might seem wofully incongruous, yet to our eyes it is supremely satisfying — *for we did it.*

Yes, the fifth story of that old warehouse asserts itself like a diamond pin in a soiled and rumpled scarf, for the mansard roof with its galvanized-iron trimmings, which once made it appear no more respectable than it ought to be, has given place to a long, well-glazed, dormer window, finished on the outside with heavy timbering and rough plaster work, and fitted with swinging sashes through whose many panes the southern sun may shine without let or hinderance, save when, in summer months, a wide, striped awning parries the hottest rays. In every sense of the word it is a great window, and — as I and many another officer of the Third can testify — the comfortable, cushioned seat which runs its entire length has many attractions for a lazy, tobacco-loving man. Above the window, and crowning glory of all, a straight and slender spar points skyward, from which, on sunny days, floats a great, white flag, bearing in mid-field the blue Maltese cross, on which the figure " 3 " is displayed: for the present Third is the successor of a "fighting regiment," and we proudly preserve the old corps' device and the traditions that go with it.

So much for the *outside* of our nightly gathering-place.

Within-doors the effect is even more surprising, for the four long and dusty flights of dimly-lighted stairs give no hint of the cheery quarters up to which they lead the way. Once they had their termination in a loft — a bare, rough, unfinished loft; but we have changed all that, and now it would be hard to find at any club in town a cosier spot. Thirty feet from side to side the great room stretches, and twice that from front to rear; ample room, yet none too much for our needs, for our friends are many, and the times are not infrequent when we find even these quarters crowded. At the southern end, almost from wall to wall, extends the long window, with its softly cushioned seat — a vantage point that never lacks for tenants. Midway of one side wall the great fireplace yawns, waiting for the sharp, cold nights when the load of logs upon its iron fire-dogs shall be called upon to send the smoke wreathing and curling up the chimney's broad and blackened throat.

Above the wide mantel-shelf are crossed two faded colors, hanging mòtionless from their staves, save when some stray current of air idly stirs their tarnished, golden fringes: "Old Glory," with its stripes and star-sown field, is one; the other, the white banner of

the Commonwealth, beneath whose crest the
ever-watchful Indian stands guard. In a
long, glittering row, below the mantel, hang
the polished pewter mugs, swinging expect-
antly, each upon its hook, and seeming to
say — as they flash back the sunbeams, or re-
flect the light of the fire below — "Come,
fill us, empty us: and have done with the
worries of the day!"

Furniture? Yes, there's a plenty. Front-
ing the hospitable fireplace a long, oaken table
stands sturdily upon its solid legs, as indeed
it *must* — for often and often, when the fire
is crackling, it has to bear a load of lazy soldiers, who delight to roost along its edge and
match the logs in smoking: chairs enough
there are to be sure, but somehow there
comes a greater sense of comfort and ease to
one who perches on a table's edge. Beneath
a trophy of Arab swords and spears stands
the bookcase, on whose shelves the literature
ranges from Tibdall, Upton, and the long
and ever-lengthening series of solemn black
"Reports," to the crazy yarns of Lever, and
the books whose backs bear the names of
Captain King and Kipling. In one corner
the upright piano, in its ebony case, has its

station — and here our lieutenant-colonel holds command undisputed, for his touch upon the ivory keys can make the rafters ring with the airs that we all know and like the best; not far away, a pillowed lounge stands waiting for an occupant; and all about are scattered small tables, ready for the whist players. A few rugs and half a dozen deer-skins litter the floor; while here and there, along the walls, are fixed the heads and horns of elk and mountain sheep — for there are two among us who spend their leaves each year far in the West, amid the big game. Everywhere there are pictures: engravings, etchings, colored prints, and, last and most of all, photographs by the dozen, and almost by the hundred — for we of the Third always have borne a reputation for unflinchingly facing the camera.

This is " The Battery."

Yes, this is The Battery, and here you may drop in on any night with the certainty of finding a pipe and a mug, and good fellows in plenty with whom to pass the time of day and pick to bits the latest thing in the way of general orders.

What gave it the name? I cannot tell.

I only know that we always have spoken of it thus, perhaps because of the shining brass howitzers that stand on end, one on either side of the chimney-piece. At odd times, to be sure, we have talked of giving the old sky-parlor some more high-sounding title, but the years have gone by without ever our getting to it, and the name which first was thrown at the place has stuck to it. And now, since Pollard, our junior major, has used his influence in municipal politics to have the name of the court changed to correspond, the chances are that " The Battery" it will be, so long as the Third stands *first* in the service — which, we fondly hope, will be always.

One night in December we had been having a battalion drill at the armory, and — an occurrence by no means uncommon — a goodly array of officers from other regiments had come over to see our work, and openly congratulate us upon the beauty of it, while secretly hugging to their hearts the conviction that *they* could do the same things twice as well. When the armory part of the programme had been put out of the way, we all adjourned to The Battery, and there — after Sam had relieved the visitors of their heavy,

military coats, which he folded and stacked
upon a chair, like so many cheap ulsters in a
ready-made clothing store — our guests went
'round the room on the usual tour of inspection, while those of us who had not detailed
ourselves to act as guides helped Sam to load
the long table with pewters.

Presently all the mugs had been filled with
beer, and at a glance from the colonel we
gathered about him. " Gentlemen of the
Third," he said, raising his froth-capped mug,
" our guests ! "— and upon this hint we drank
heartily, and very willingly indeed, to the visit-
ing officers whom we had with us. Then Major
Wilson, the senior of our guests, proposed
our healths, and with the conclusion of this
simple ceremony we laid aside all formality,
and scattered ourselves over the room, while
Sam passed around the tray of pipes and the
great Japanese jar of cut-plug.

Each equipped with corn-cob and mug —
for our tastes are not luxurious, and beer and
tobacco amply satisfy them — we split up
into groups, and as the smoke-cloud became
more dense the talk grew louder, until the
clatter of mugs, the humming monotone of
many voices, and the frequent bursts of

laughter combined to drown the sound of the hissing and crackling logs in the fireplace.

"Is that one of your trophies, Major?" asked Kenryck, of the brigade staff, speaking to Sawin, our surgeon, and nodding up at a huge pair of moose horns upon the wall above the mantel.

"No, that's a contribution from the colonel," replied Sawin, *alias* "Bones," setting down his mug and wiping his mustache as he spoke. "Langforth and I plead guilty to the slaughter of most of these horns and hides, for we're the 'mighty hunters' of this aggregation, but *that* pair of antlers fell to someone else's rifle. Splendid pair, eh? There's a sort of story goes with 'em, too. Ask the colonel."

"Yes, there *is* a story connected with that pair," said Colonel Elliott, who, from his side of the table, overheard the doctor's suggestion. He rose, transferred his chair and mug to a position next Kenryck, and continued: "In fact, when we began to fit up this place, we made it a rule not to admit among the decorations anything which didn't have a history of some sort. So, you see, The Battery is rather an interesting establishment, and if any of us had time or taste for that sort of thing we could get up a good-sized book without having to go outside these walls to hunt for material."

" It's a mighty interesting outfit— the whole of it," said Kenryck, glancing up and down the long room, and noting the collection of odds and ends upon the walls and in every nook and corner. " We're pretty well fixed, up at *our* headquarters, but we've nothing so homelike as this. The general often says that he enjoys nothing more than an inspection of the Third, with a 'wind-up' afterwards up here. Possibly you've noticed that, on occasions of that sort, his whole staff is apt to come with him."

" Yes," said the colonel dryly, remembering the extra cases of beer which have to be laid in against such emergencies as an official visit from the brigade staff; "yes, I've noticed it. It's very flattering to us, I'm sure."

Kenryck must have been aware of something in the colonel's tone, for he promptly drew upon his reserve supply of tact and said, " Do you mind telling me the story of those horns? It's worth hearing, I know, for Sawin put me up to asking for it."

"It's an old story to 'Bones,'" said the colonel, adding, as Sam passed him, "Break into another case, Sam, and then chuck a couple more sticks into the fire."

"It must be a good one, then, or he never would have let me in for it," remarked Kenryck.

"I wouldn't be too sure of that," said the colonel, laughing; "the doctor's capable of almost anything inhuman, and he may be paying off an old score, for all *you* know, by letting you in for a twenty-minute bore. 'Bones,' what's your grudge against Kenryck?"—but the surgeon had joined a group at another table, and so the colonel, getting no reply to his question, went on: "Do you see that little ivory plate fastened to the shield on which the horns are mounted? Well, that bears an inscription something like this:

John Harnden Pender, C.S.N.,
to
Henry Elliott, U.S.N.
Jan'y 29th, 1871.

" And the story is not a long one :

" My father was interested in shipping, and at the breaking out of the war he owned quite a respectable little fleet of vessels. Most of them were employed in coastwise trade, but he had something like three or four square-riggers winging it back and forth between here and England — and sometimes, though rarely, one of his vessels would make a longer voyage, to Bombay, or 'round the Horn to Frisco. Ah, those were the good old days ! when the harbor was crowded with shipping, and at least every other ship flew the stars and stripes," and the colonel raised his mug to his lips, as if drinking to the past glories of our merchant marine.

" It must have been a pleasant sight," said Kenryck, in the pause incident to this operation. " I'm a young man, and can't remember that time, but now-days it's sort of pathetic to see the harbor filled with huge steamers under foreign bunting, while here and there along the docks a few wretched little schooners represent our maritime dignity."

" Yes, it's pathetic enough," said the colonel, " but it's more humiliating than pathetic. However, we can't go into the discussion of what knocked in the head our ocean carrying trade without running foul of politics, and politics are barred, up here in The Battery.

" Well, to get back to my story : my father naturally had quite an acquaintance among Englishmen, and in Liverpool there was an old party named McClintock, with whom, in particular, he had very extensive dealings. In course of time he and my governor became great chums, and finally it got so that once in two years, and sometimes oftener, one or the other of them would cross the pond, nominally on business, but really for a visit. Lord! how well I can remember old David McClintock — 'Mac,' my governor used to call him. Square-built and stocky, hearty and bluff, intellectually sure, but *awfully* slow — he certainly was a man to make an impression, for he represented a type with which we are not over-familiar on this side the water. I can't forget how he used to laugh at the governor's yarns : ten minutes would go by without any sign of comprehension from him ; then he would begin to shake ; and finally the spasm would pass away, leaving him gasping for breath, and scarlet in the face. Really, Kenryck, I used to worry about old Mac, at those times, for his internal mirth was something awful, and it made me fear for his blood-vessels."

"I know a man like that," put in Kenryck, "and it makes me nervous to be near him when anything amuses him. But somehow, Colonel, he seems to get more satisfaction from his silent way of laughing than most men do who laugh out loud."

"The last time that McClintock came over to this side," continued the colonel, after a glance at the antlers and the faded colors crossed below them, "was in '60. He brought his daughter with him — a pretty girl, too; about eighteen at that time. I'm not making any official statement, Kenryck, but I've always thought that the two old gentlemen had put their heads together with an idea of arranging an international marriage, in which one of the leading parts was to have been assigned to me. It may be, though, that my suspicions have been unfounded, for there certainly never was anything *said* about it. Anyway, if either old

Mac or my governor had been indulging in
any schemes of that sort, they were destined
to disappointment, because, firstly, I had
reasons for thinking that a certain little
Boston girl was about the proper thing for
me, and secondly — and a clincher on
obstacle number one — little Bess McClintock took a strong dislike to me. Never quite
understood *why*," said the colonel, meditatively tugging at his mustache, " and don't
yet. I thought that most girls rather liked me,
in those days. Probably she saw through the
whole business — for she was a level-headed
little chap — and got huffed at the idea of
being ' managed.' "

" Yes? " said Kenryck, with a rising in-
flection which hinted at a lack of any very
lively interest in what was being said, and
led the colonel to continue : " Well, all this
is neither here nor there, Kenryck, and you
must pardon me for getting away from my
yarn. But a pipe and a good listener always
tempt me to talk along rather aimlessly.

" When old Mac and his daughter came
for their visit, we had with us a young fellow named Pender, from Charleston. He
was the son of a man with whom my father,

in the course of his southern trade, had a
very considerable amount of business, and he
had come north to settle up some matter or
other—*just* what, I forget. Gad! but he was
a hot-headed little chap! At that time, you
know, feeling was beginning to run pretty
high, and I had to do some pretty sharp
manœuvering in order to keep peace in our
house, for my father was uncompromisingly
patriotic, and even went so far as to favor
abolition, while Pender — well, Pender was
a southerner to the core, and went in, neck-
or-nothing, for the 'Sacred Institution,' and
States' Rights, and all those things over which
later we went to fighting. It was a cheerful
day for me when he finished up his business
and went back home, for though in some
ways I liked him well enough, yet while he
was at our house I never sat down to a
meal without an uncomfortable feeling that
at any minute some chance remark might
fire a train that would bring about a general
explosion.

"It always seems strange to me, when I
remember the radical difference in tempera-
ment, but old McClintock developed quite
a liking for Pender. To be sure, he didn't

fall in with all of his ideas, but he had a certain amount of sympathy for the southern view of the situation, and he used to reply to my governor's criticisms of Pender with, ' Eh, but he's a spirited lad, ye know — a spirited lad. Bide a wee, Elliott, bide a wee. Years will give the boy more wisdom.'

" Well, in due time old Mac and his daughter went, and the war came," went on Colonel Elliott, after a pause which lessened by half a pint the contents of his mug. " I went out with the ' Old Regiment,' and for the better part of four years I was a stranger to this part of the country. When finally I came home for good and all, I found my father retired from business, and in feeble health. His little fleet had disappeared. For some of the vessels which once composed it the *Alabama* could have accounted, and the general feeling of insecurity in shipping circles had caused him to sell the rest. In '66 the governor died, and about a month afterwards I received a letter from old Mac, in which he expressed the deepest sorrow, and said that I must come to see him in Liverpool, since he had determined never again to visit the States.

" Pender I had lost sight of, and almost had forgotten, for with my father's retirement from business I lost touch with many of our old friends and acquaintances, and besides, the war rather cleaned the slate of our southern connections."

" There must have been a funny state of affairs in business, right after the war," observed Kenryck, making a gallant attempt to conceal a yawn, and, by the aid of his sheltering mug, succeeding in his effort.

" There *was*," said the colonel, "and for some time afterwards, too. It took more than one year for northern business men to forget some slight irregularities which showed themselves in the course of trade about that period.

" Well, after I'd hung up my sword, had my commission and discharge properly framed, and told my war stories to everyone who could be induced to listen to them, I began to look about for an occupation. I ended up by drifting into marine insurance.

" One forenoon, early in '71 — the 29th of January, according to that little plate up there on the horns — I was sitting in my office and wrestling with the question whether I should lunch at half-past twelve or wait until one. Business happened to be quiet then, you see, and so I was able to give a good deal of thought to minor details like that. I had just decided in favor of half-past twelve, when a messenger came in and informed me that a certain Captain Pender was very desirous of having me come to the county jail to see him. Beyond this bald statement I could get no information except that the man who had sent for me was locked up on a pretty serious charge — just what, or how grave, the messenger didn't know.

"This bit of information made me forget all about the lunch question, and I wasted no time in getting over to the jail. And there, safely tucked away behind the bars, I found my Charleston acquaintance of '60 — fuming and boiling with rage, and with the maddest kind of rage, too. Why, Pender was no lamb, at best, but when I got to him, that day, it was an even chance whether he'd kick down the walls of his cell or bite off the iron bars of the grated door. And his *language* — oh, it was sublime! I was in active service for four years, Kenryck, and gained some knowledge of the power of words; I've stood

by and listened to an army teamster's remarks to a team of balky mules; I've even
had occasion myself to make brief addresses
to company skulkers whom I've caught modestly stealing to the rear; but I *never* knew
how much could be got out of our mother
tongue until I stood outside of that cell door,
and heard Pender tell what he thought of
the man who had managed to get him shut
up there."

"Well, what had he done?" asked Kenryck, as the colonel paused to signal for Sam,
by rapping with his empty mug upon the
table. "Had he shot that moose out of sea-
son?"

"Bah! no, he was in for a worse shooting
affair than *that*," replied the colonel, still
smiling at the remembrance of Pender's outburst. "After he'd cursed himself out of
breath, and had been compelled, from sheer
exhaustion, to seat himself upon the edge of
his cot, I managed to get at the story of the
whole trouble. It ran something like this:

"When the 'late unpleasantness' began,
Pender, as you may have guessed, lost no
time in taking a hand in the game, and as his
tastes led him in that direction he entered

the confederate naval service — such as it
was. He was a capable officer, without any
doubt, and promotion came rapidly in his
case, for, a little over two years after the
war had begun, he had reached the rank of
captain. Now the other side never was very
strong in the naval branch of the service, and
after a time Pender — who never was any
too patient — began to fidget and fuss because he couldn't seem to get a vessel that
suited him, and, what was worse, could see no
prospect of having one provided for him.
Well, what do you suppose he did ? You've
heard of the *Halifax* affair ? "

"No," said Kenryck, "can't say that I
have — or, if I have, I don't recall it now."

" It was as plucky an exhibition as was
put up by either side during the whole war
— about the same sort of exploit that some
of our fellows performed when they captured
the locomotive inside the confederate lines,"
said the colonel, taking the replenished mug
which Sam had brought him. " Pender, as
I have said, wanted a ship, — and wanted it
badly, — so, as the confederacy wasn't *building* many at that time, he calmly sat down and
gave his brains a chance, and ended up by

figuring out that it would be comparatively easy, and superlatively cheap, to come up north and help himself to one.

"And he *did* it, too, by Jove!" said the colonel, bringing his fist down with a thump upon the oaken table. "He just took his pick among the officers whom he knew, and selected an even half-dozen, besides himself, to work out his little idea. One by one they slipped inside our lines, and finally they all got together safely up here in Boston. It must have been nuts for Pender — the secret and solemn conspirators' meetings, the planning and plotting of when and how, and the stiff seasoning of danger which gave spice to the whole undertaking. He told me himself that he gladly would give ten years of his life to go through with it again.

"At that time there was a line of steamers running between this port and the 'Provinces,' and the vessels composing it were all first-class, seaworthy craft; for, as probably you know, there's pretty nasty weather to be met, off there to the east'ard. Now, of the whole lot the *Halifax* was the best, and our government had had an eye on her for some time, for she had in her the making of a

good gun-boat, and would have come up very
handily to blockading requirements. But Pender's eye was just as keen as Uncle Sam's,
and Pender's motions were a great deal more
sudden, and so the *Halifax* never attained
the dignity of a place in our navy; for, when
she left her dock to begin her last voyage
‘Down East,’ she bore upon her passenger-
list seven ornamentally fictitious names,
under cover of which travelled Captain John
Harnden Pender, C.S.N., and the six choice
spirits whom he had chosen to back him up.”

“So he stole her, did he?” exclaimed
Kenryck, at last beginning to take a little
interest in the story.

“*Stole* her! no, indeed,” said Colonel
Elliott, in a tone of rebuke. “That's hardly
a gentlemanly way to put it. In war you
don't steal things: you *capture* them. Iden-
tity in ideas, you know, but dissimilarity in
terms. Pender would be hurt if he should
happen to hear his exploit classed as larceny.
Well, the *Halifax* went churning along on her
course, and until she was well outside the
bay there was nothing unusual in the conduct
of her passengers. But when she had a
good offing, there came a transformation

scene; and, all of a sudden, the men in the pilot-house and engine-room found themselves looking into the barrels of a very respectable number of navy revolvers.

"There wasn't much chance for argument. One of the engineers tried it on, but he only got shot for his pains — and the results in his case seemed to discourage the others. In short, the job was done neatly and in a thoroughly workmanlike way, and it took, all told, not much over half an hour to change the course of the *Halifax* from a northerly to a southerly one. Sounds easy, doesn't it? Well, it *was*."

"So they got clean away with her?" said the colonel's listener. "It hardly seems possible!"

"Yes, at first they played in luck, and got away with her right enough," said Colonel Elliott; "but their luck failed to hold, and off the coast of the Carolinas they had to go blundering plump into the blockading squadron. Sandy as Pender was, he couldn't fight his ship with Colt's revolvers, so, when he found himself in a fair way to be pocketed by two or three of our cruisers, he made the best of a bad mess, headed the poor old

Halifax for the shore, sent her, head on and
at full speed, upon the sands, and left her
there ablaze from stem to stern. I don't know
what he said during the operation, but I'd bet
something that if his words were put into
print they'd have to be bound in asbestos or
some other non-inflammable material. Well,
it *was* hard luck, and — Union veteran though
I am — I'm damned if I can help feeling sorry
that Pender didn't get away with his ship!
I'd have liked to see what he'd have done
with her."

The colonel reached for the tobacco-jar,
filled a corn-cob, lighted it, and then went
on : " After this unsuccessful experiment of
his, he failed to get many more chances, for
in some scrimmage or other he managed to
get badly used up, and didn't get fairly into
shape until the war was nearly over. When
finally the Confederacy went down he was
one of those who couldn't philosophically
accept the result of the struggle, and in an
aimless sort of way he drifted over to England. There he brought up at Liverpool, and
in the course of events happened again upon
old David McClintock. Well, after this he
had everything his own way, for the old man

completely surrendered to him. First, he went to stay at Mac's house ; next, he went into business with him ; and finally he made love to Bess and married her. He couldn't have wasted much time over it all, either, for it all had taken place when he showed up, here in Boston, in '71. But that was Pender all over. 'Eh, but he was a spirited lad, ye know.' "

Kenryck laughed at this application of old McClintock's words, and the colonel, who had stopped to pack more closely the tobacco in his pipe, continued: " He had come to Boston on a matter of business, and was about to look me up when he found himself put behind the bars, almost as soon as he had stepped off the New York train. How did *that* come about? Very simply. It seems that he had met, at some hotel in Liverpool, a Boston man who still was rabid on the war question. The fellow wasn't a veteran, but was one of those who staid at home and *shouted* for the Union — and they are the ones who keep the hatchet longest unburied. Somehow he managed to get into a discussion with Pender, and displayed such a lamentable lack of tact that, before he half

knew it, the little ex-rebel had knocked him
flat, and had repeated the operation twice
running. It was a sort of argument to which
he was unaccustomed, and he seemed offended
at it."

" A bit put out, eh ? " said Kenryck, with
a grin at the matter-of-fact way in which
Colonel Elliott made this latter statement.

" More *knocked* out," replied the colonel,
with an answering smile. " I'm not wasting
much sympathy over him, for he wasn't
exactly the style of man I like. Why, Kenryck, instead of getting up and going for
Pender, he slunk off quietly and, all by himself, hatched up a dirty little scheme for
squaring the account without running further
risk of getting a black eye.

" In some way he'd got hold of Pender's
war record, and, learning that he shortly was
to come across to this side, he made off, post-
haste, for Boston, where he set to work very
industriously to arrange a proper reception
for the man who had presumed to punch his
patriotic nose. I must admit that he did his
work very nicely, and the first results probably were quite gratifying to him, for about as
soon as Pender set foot in this town he was

arrested under a warrant charging piracy, and murder on the high seas, and pretty much every cheerful sort of crime and mis-demeanor, all on account of his little esca-pade on the *Halifax*, eight years before. It was at this stage of the game that I was called upon to take a hand."

"Why, I'm blessed if I can see —" began Kenryck.

"How the charges could be supported, eh?" said the colonel, finishing his ques-tion for him. "Well, they couldn't be, and weren't. The case never came to trial, for we were able to show the facts of the matter in the proper light, and with less trouble than I had dared hope. But I had to trot up bail to the amount of fifteen thousand before I could put Pender into more congenial quarters, and, first and last, I wasted the better part of a week in getting the complications disentangled."

"And *then* what happened?" asked Ken-ryck, with a grin of anticipation. "I sup-pose Pender took the first chance to knock the head off his man?"

"*Wouldn't* he have!" said Colonel Elliott, with something like a sigh of relief at the thought that his peppery little southerner was safe in Liverpool again, and unlikely ever to cause him further trouble. "Why, Kenryck, I honestly thought he'd be back again in jail inside of a week, and for *real* murder, too. But, luckily, our friend the informer found it convenient to leave town as soon as he saw the turn affairs were taking, and so the gutters didn't run with blood, after all.

"Well, things calmed down, and in time Pender cooled off sufficiently to attend to his business. But he worried the life half out of me by thanking me over and over again, at all sorts of times and in all sorts of places, for what he was pleased to call my 'soldierly magnanimity.' At last, and just as he was beginning to become rather a bore, he took himself off on a hunting trip, somewhere up Canada way, and that was the last I saw of him, for he went back to England by way of Montreal. But after he'd been gone about three weeks I had a reminder of him, in the shape of that pair of horns, which, with his card attached, came to me by express. I had them mounted on the shield, and put that plate upon them, partly because they recall rather an odd experience, and partly to keep myself in mind that the war is over."

"Now, that's quite a story," said Kenryck, as the colonel paused. "I should think, though, that you would keep the horns at home. They are a splendid pair, and the story makes them doubly valuable."

"I had them in my hall for years," said the colonel, "but when we set out to fit up The Battery here, I chipped them in as part of my contribution, for that space of wall, in there between the colors, seemed made on purpose for them. But those antlers are not my only reminder of Pender's gratitude," he continued, taking out his pocket-book and extracting from it a photograph of a bald-headed, pudgy-faced infant, " for here's a picture of a young Liverpool citizen who rejoices in the name of Henry Elliott Pender. He's Pender's third, and he's bound to grow up into a terrible little rebel, for his father is still unreconstructed. Doesn't look very formidable, does he? I'm ready, though, to bet my commission against a corporal's warrant that, one of these days, I'll have a namesake in either Her Majesty's army or navy, for the little rascal comes of fighting stock, and blood will tell."

"Apparently the doctor *didn't* have a grudge to settle," said Kenryck, handing back the photograph. Then, after disposing of what little beer was left in his pewter, he got upon his feet, saying, "Well, Colonel, I hope I'll have the luck to get up here often, for I want to hear the stories that go with the rest of these odds and ends."

"Hello!" said Colonel Elliott, glancing at the clock. "Is it so late as *that!* Trust I've not bored you; you're too good a listener to frighten away."

Kenryck went to rescue his overcoat from the fast diminishing pile upon the chair, while the colonel, pipe in hand, took up a position near the door, to bid good-night to our departing guests. By twos and threes our visitors left us, and then the colonel, as the last descending footfall echoed faintly up the long staircase, turned and glanced at the disorderly array of empty mugs. " I venture to assert," he said, with a laugh, "that there are worse places for story-telling than The Battery. Judging by appearances, I think it doubtful if there's been a *dry* yarn told to-night, up here."

"Twenty-two, twenty-four, twenty-six," counted Sam, as he made the rounds of the deserted tables. "Twenty-six mugs t' clean an' shine up! Wal, 'twan't sich a bad evenin' a'ter all." And we left him gathering up the tarnished pewters, and swearing strange, New England oaths — "B'gosh!" and "I swan!" and "Gol darn!" — at the prospect of the morrow's polishing.

ONE RECORD

REGIMENTAL ROLLS

ONE RECORD

ON THE

REGIMENTAL ROLLS.

"VERY pretty," said the colonel, "very pretty, indeed. Quite up to *our* standard, eh, Jack? Guard looks small, though, — doesn't it? — to one who's used to seeing twenty-four files paraded." The colonel and I had got leave for a couple of weeks to run down to Old Point to see the heavy gun practice, and now we stood watching the new guard as it marched away to relieve the old details.

Yes, it *was* pretty, all of it, — very pretty indeed, — and I felt repaid for the early breakfast we had taken in order to get over to the fort in time for the ceremony. The surroundings made a fitting frame for the picture : before us lay the broad, green floor of the level parade, its carpet of short-cropped turf still glistening with the morning dew; the angular lines of the great, ungainly barracks somehow looked less harsh in the warm sunshine; and the officers' quarters, half hidden beneath the scrubby oaks and overhanging willows, looked cosey and comfortable — and almost too homelike for such a place.

While the gray, sod-capped walls of the old fort still were ringing with the quickstep played by the four smart trumpeters who led the guard in its march, we turned and left the parade, loitering for a moment at the place where the old guns — relics of York-town, Saratoga, and many another by-gone siege and battle — lie sullen and dumb, while the green mould of long years gathers ever more thickly upon cascabel, chase, and trunnion. " Back numbers," said the colonel, half to himself, as he stooped to read the inscription deeply graven in the metal of an old field-piece, " back numbers, all of them. ' Captured at Yorktown '— and that was more than a hundred years ago ! Well, those who won and those who lost are under ground now, and the old gun's dead, too. It has said its last word."

We sauntered away, through the echoing

archway, and across the drawbridge which spans the green and quiet water of the wide ditch; and as we slowly walked past the water battery, with its long row of grim, black Rodmans frowning out upon the bay — each in its vaulted casemate — like so many kennelled watch-dogs, the colonel broke the silence with, "Do you know, Jack, I don't care particularly about watching the firing to-day? The pounding we got yesterday was infernal. I hope this country can steer clear of war until we've perfected the pneumatic gun."

"Well, I don't know," said I. "Wouldn't that seem too much like fighting with bean-blowers?"

"It wouldn't much resemble the fighting in the old days — and that's a fact," replied the colonel, kicking into the ditch a pebble from the gravelled roadway, and smiling at the sudden scattering of a school of little fish, caused by the unexpected splash. "I'm not so sure, after all, that I'm in a hurry for the time to arrive when some fellow, ten miles or so away, can free a lot of compressed air, and by means of it drop half a barrel of dynamite in my vicinity — without even so much as a puff of smoke to show which way I ought to turn to bow my acknowledgments. I've an idea, old man, that a little occurrence of that sort would scatter even the gallant Third about as completely and expeditiously as my pebble disorganized those minnows."

A few steps more brought us beyond the last of the curving line of casemates, and as we turned towards the hotel the colonel said, " I feel that I'm growing old, for now-a-days even a little heavy gun firing makes my ears ache, and anything *over* a little bores me. Thirty years ago I didn't mind it so much as I do now. *Thirty years ago?* Why, Jack, I can't realize it ! But it must be that : yes, '61 from '91 ; that makes it — and it makes me an old man, too."

" Nonsense ! " said I, laughing, for in all the Third there is no younger-hearted man than the colonel who commands it. " It makes you nothing of the sort. In '61 you were nineteen ; add thirty to that — and it leaves you still on the sunny side of fifty. See here, Colonel ; on our rolls we have seven hundred men, and some few over — how many are there among them who could down you to-day ? "

" Not many, if I *do* say it," replied the colonel, with his usual modesty, drawing himself up and stretching out one long arm, to gaze contemplatively at the sinewy wrist and compact bunch of knuckles with which it terminated. " But all that only goes to show how well preserved I am, for I *am* an old man, in spite of what you say. Confound you, Jack! Can't you let a veteran have the satisfaction of *feeling* venerable and antique?"

" All right," I replied, laughing again. " You're my commanding officer, and if you order me to consider you a relic, why, I must, I suppose. Perhaps it may comfort you to know that the boys conversationally refer to you as ' the old man.' "

" There, enough of that," said the colonel, as we stepped upon the planking of the long piazza. " What's the use of discussing my infirmities? Now, how shall we kill time this forenoon? Billiards? No, hardly; it's too good a day to waste indoors. I'll tell you what we'll do, my boy: we'll go over to Hampton and take a look at the old fellows in the ' Home.' Which shall it be, drive or walk?"

"Walk," said I promptly, as I felt the fresh, salt breeze come stealing in from off the water; "yes, we'll walk, unless at your advanced age you don't feel quite up to the exertion."

"Walk it is, then," said the colonel, ignoring my attempt to pay proper deference to his accumulated years. "Just wait a second, though; I must fill my pockets before we start. I like to lay a trail of cigars when I go among the old boys," and with this he disappeared into the hotel, from which he emerged a moment later, bearing a paper of weeds which, he explained, were not rankly poisonous for open-air smoking, though they might involve some unpleasant consequences if lighted within-doors.

We set off at a swinging gait along the road, and in something less than half an hour found ourselves at the entrance of the well-kept grounds in which are clustered the buildings of the Soldiers' Home. It is a beautiful place, that quiet spot by the southern sea, and I never could tire of strolling along its flower-bordered walks, and among its sunny nooks and corners. And yet, even in the midst of the brightest sun-

shine, one cannot escape the thought that
the hundreds upon hundreds of gray-haired,
feeble men who throng these grounds have
come here, after all, only to *die*, and are
waiting — waiting until it shall be their turn
to be carried out to the great graveyard
which, with its acres and acres of white head-
stones, lies but a few short steps outside the
gates. It is a thought that somehow seems
to dim the sunshine a little, and though the
place is wonderfully picturesque, and wears
an outward air of ease and comfort, yet I, for
one, never can be there without feeling
almost awe-stricken at the remembrance of
what it all means.

"Now, Jack," said the colonel, as we
walked leisurely along the broad, hard roadway, which runs parallel with the blue
waters of Hampton Roads, "keep an eye
out for 'blue Maltees,' for that's the particular breed of cats we're after."

"All right," I replied, interpreting this
command to mean that I was to be on the
watch for veterans wearing the badge of the
old 19th Army Corps — the blue Maltese
cross; a device which we of the Third still
retain, in memory of the days when the

"Old Regiment" won its renown. "White diamonds, red crescents, and stars of every color seem to be plenty, Colonel, but, so far as I can see, 'Maltees' are at a premium."

"Oh, we shall find one," said the colonel, "we surely shall find one. There are rows upon rows of them lying quietly over yonder," with a nod towards the flag floating above the cemetery, "but they are not yet *all* mustered out. There's one now, over on that bench. See him?"

Yes, I saw him; a short, wiry man; a man with whitened hair, keen gray eyes, a sharply-pointed nose, and a clean-shaven face whose every line and wrinkle betokened shrewdness and native wit. At the first brief glance I knew him for a Yankee, a thoroughbred old New Englander.

He was sittting alone upon the bench, with one knee drawn up and held by his clasped hands. Upon his cap he wore the blue Maltese cross we had been seeking, and on the breast of his faded and loosely fitting army blouse hung a simple medal of bronze. Into one corner of his mouth was stuck a quaintly carved, briar-wood pipe, and as he tranquilly sat there, blowing from his thin lips an occasional puff of smoke, he seemed contented with himself and the world in general — and I somehow thought that in his expression I saw something different from the air of hopelessness which had been so sadly common to the many old soldiers we had passed before we happened upon him.

"Hello, comrade," said the colonel, walking towards the bench on which the old fellow sat, and throwing open his coat to bring into view the enamelled corps badge pinned upon his waistcoat, "how goes it with you?"

"Fust-rate," replied the veteran, without bothering to remove his pipe from its resting place. "How be ye?" he went on, speaking with a sharp, nasal twang which at once opened my heart to him — for he *was* a Yankee, and I love the honest, hardy old stock that comes from among the New England hills and valleys. "I see *you* was in th' ol' 19th, too," said he, moving over to the end of the seat. "Set ye down an' be comf'table."

"Yes, I went out with the —th Massachusetts and saw the thing through," said the colonel, seating himself next his

new-found friend and leaving vacant for me
one end of the bench. " What was your
regiment ? "

" Burdett's Batt'ry, New Hampshire," replied the old fellow, with a critical side-
glance at the colonel; " an' if ye was in
th' Massachusetts —th ye won't have no
trouble in rememberin' how our guns use'-
ter sound, neither."

" Lord ! I should *say* not," said the colonel,
turning to me with, " This comes to pretty
much the same thing as meeting an old acquaintance, Jack, for Burdett's Battery was
one of the best in our division, and the ' Old
Regiment' has supported it more times than
one. Yes, indeed," he went on, as he reached
into his pocket for his cigars, " I 've listened
to your music many a day. Good music,
too, it was. The infantry does the work —
but sometimes guns are mighty comforting
companions."

" You *bet* they be," said the old artillery-
man, shaking the ashes from his pipe and
taking a cigar from the paper which the
colonel held towards him. " Thank ye. A
pipe's my reg'lar smoke, but once 'n a while I
kind o' like t' change off onto a cigar. Yis,

I was in Burdett's Light Batt'ry, an' was mustered out a sargint."

"What brought you down here?" asked the colonel, handing a match to the old soldier. "Down on your luck a bit, eh?"

"No-o, not exackly," returned the veteran, as he smartly drew the match across his thigh after the manner of one who had acquired the habit in active service. Glancing quickly around, and seeing that we were alone — for the nearest group was gathered beside an old siege gun, some fifty yards away — he lowered his voice a trifle and said, "Fact is, I ain't *obliged* t' board down here, an', strickly speakin', I s'pose I hadn't oughter be here at all. Ye see, when I'm home I live up Swanzey way — that's up in New Hampshire, an' not sech an orful way from th' Massachusetts line. I'm able t' git along tol'ably comf'table up there, with one odd job an' another, but this fall I kind o' took it inter my head that I'd like t' spend th' winter south, an' I managed it, too. So here I be. Nex' spring, though, when things gits all thawed out up north, I guess I'll move along up agin t' see th' folks, for this is a terrible shif'less sort o' country, down here, an' I wouldn't want t' stay here for a stiddy thing."

" I see how it is," laughed the colonel, understanding that this confession was made because the old sergeant hated to have it thought that he had been driven by want to accept the government's hospitality. "You're playing it foxy on Uncle Sam for a little vacation."

" I s'pose 'taint quite right, lookin' at it in some ways," said the old gunner apologetically. "But I spent four years south *workin'* for our Uncle Samuel, an' it *doos* seem 's if I might rest here one winter at his expense, 'specially sence I'm a sort o' namesake o' his. Besides, 'taint like it might be 'f I was drawin' a penshin, neither, for I never tried t' git one, though there's plenty o' men takin' dollars out o' th' treas'ry that aint got no better claim than I have."

" You're decorated, I see," said I, nodding towards the medal upon his breast. " Isn't that the ' Medal of Honor' that is awarded only by vote of Congress ? "

" Yis, that's *jest* what it is," replied the sergeant, unpinning it and handing it over for my inspection. " Guess 'taint worth

much; it's nothin' but copper. Seems 's if
the gov'ment don't calc'late t' spend much
on them sort o' fixin's. I got it 'bout three
years ago."

" 'To Sergeant Samuel Farwell,' " I read
aloud, " ' October 29th, 1864.' Do you mean
to say, sergeant, that you waited twenty-
four years to obtain recognition of your
bravery ?"

" Wal, there warn't no one t' blame 'cept
me," remarked my New Englander, taking
the medal from the colonel, to whom I had
passed it, and fastening it again in its place
upon the breast of his blouse. " Ye have t'
apply for them things yourself, an' git all
sorts o' document'ry evidence t' back ye up.
It makes consid'able bother, fust an' last,
an' I'll be darned 'f I'd go through all th'
fuss agin for a peck on ' em."

" Tell us about it," said the colonel, who
seemed amused at the light in which Farwell
regarded his decoration. " What did you
get it for ? "

" What did I git it for ? " repeated the old
gunner, with a twinkle in his gray eye and a
twitching of the muscles at the corner of
his mouth which warned us that he medi-

tated some outbreak of Yankee wit. " What *for ?* Oh, 'cause — what with Odd Fellers, an' hose companies, an' Sons o' Vet'rans — there wasn't many people in town that didn't have a medal o' some description, an' I got this one so 's t' be able t' shine with th' rest on 'em."

" Pshaw ! I don't mean *that*," said the colonel, with a laugh in which I joined, " What did you *do* to get it?"

" " Why, I thought I'd told ye," said the old fellow, with the twinkle still visible in his eye. " I *applied* for it, an' put in my documents t' prove I warn't lyin' — an' ol' Cap'n Burdett helped me consid'able by speakin' t' our member o' Congress 'bout it."

" No, no, *no !*" said the colonel, laughing again, " that's not what I want, either. That medal of yours is awarded only for distinguished bravery ; now, what was the service that made you eligible to receive it?"

" What did th' gov'nment give it t' me for? ye mean," said the sergeant, allowing himself a smile at the fun he had had with us. " Wal, 'taint goin' t' sound like much, but I'd jus' 's lives tell ye. Hello !" he interjected, " this cigar seems t' be unravellin'."

"Throw it away, then," said the colonel. "Here's another."

"Oh, no! wouldn't do that, would ye?" said the old soldier. "'Twould seem kind o' wasteful, wouldn't it? I kin tinker this one so's it'll be all right. Jes' watch me" — and with this he applied his tongue to the loosened and uncoiling wrapper, and then smoothed the well-moistened leaf securely into place, remarking, "There! she smokes as good 's new — an' there's five cents saved."

"Just about," said I, grinning, for an occasional whiff of the smoke had come my way. "How did you know?"

"Oh, I kin tell a *good* cigar, every time," remarked the veteran, liberating a prodigious puff of smoke and sniffing at it with the air of an expert judge of tobacco. "Smokin' a pipe so much haint hurt my taste for cigars a mite."

"Glad you like them," said the colonel, turning upon me an ominous frown which checked any inclination I might have had to go more deeply into the subject. "Now, about that medal?"

"Oh, yis, 'bout th' medal," said Farwell, with just one look at his cigar to see how his repairs held out. " Wal, ye mus'n't think I'm boastin' — 'cause I aint. What I done warn't no more than I've seen done time an' time agin — an' you, too, 'f you was four years with th' —th Massachusetts — an' I never'd have thought twice 'bout it 'f Cap'n Burdett hadn't kep' urgin' me on t' apply for th' medal. Pooh! 'taint nothin' but a trinket, anyway, an' it's no earthly use t' me nor anyone."

" Don't apologize. Go ahead with the story," I put in, recognizing the chance of an interesting half hour. " You didn't volunteer to tell us, you know. We asked you."

" Yes, go ahead," said the colonel, lighting a cigar, which, by the way, he took from his leather case, and not from the paper of weeds he had brought from the hotel. " I should say that things had come to a funny pass when one of the old 19th's boys is bashful about yarning to another."

" Lord! ye don't need t' think that," said the veteran. " *I* ain't bashful 'bout tellin' ye. All I was 'fraid of was that p'raps ye'd think I set myself up for bein' extra courageous — which I don't. Wal, here's all th' story there is to 't:

" We was down here in Virginia, at a place we called Three Mile Creek — 'twouldn't be many hundred miles from here, 'f a crow was t' fly it. Like enough *you* was there ? "

" Yes, I ought to remember it," said the colonel, " we lost some men there. Go on, sergeant."

" Lost some men, hey ? " said Farwell, clasping his hands behind his head, and comfortably stretching his legs out upon the gravelled path. " Wal, I guess ye'll be interested in what I'm goin' t' tell ye, 'f *that's* so. I da'say," he continued, " ye kin remember that there was some shots fired, an' that our skirmishers come back so sudden that they forgot t' bring along a few that warn't able t' walk. In fac', they *run* back, an' we in th' batt'ry thought it an almighty poor showin' on th' part o' th' infantry. But p'raps we wasn't in no position t' jedge."

" It was that sudden volley from the woods that sent the boys back in disorder," said the colonel shortly. " The skirmish line was made up of seven companies of the —th ; *my* company was one of the three in reserve."

" Why didn't they wait t' see what hit

'em?" asked the sergeant in a tone which showed traces of contempt. "D' ye think 'twas th' right thing t' skedaddle away 'thout bringin' in th' wounded?"

"No, I don't," said the colonel, flushing a little, "and it wasn't like the 'Old Regiment' to do it. But the boys were pretty well worn out and broken down by the marching and fighting we'd had, and the attack was so sudden and unexpected that it rattled them for a time. You must admit, sergeant, that we had as good a reputation as any regiment in the 19th Corps."

"Wal, *that's* so," said the old fellow, brushing an ash stain from his blouse, "an' I s'pose we noticed th' break more 'cause we warn't used t' lookin' for sich displays on your part. Now, *we* was posted up on a little knoll, ye remember, well over towards th' right; an' when th' Rebs showed up in th' open — for t' foller up you infantry fellers — we jes' dropped a round 'r two o' shell down that way, sort o' hintin' to 'em t' go back where they'd come from."

"So that was *your* battery, was it?" asked Colonel Elliott. "From the way the guns were served I always thought it was a regular battery."

"Sho! we'd been in service 'most three year then," said the veteran gunner, quickly resenting this reflection upon the efficiency of his beloved battery, "an' we'd had good practice an' lots of it, too. Would we be takin' p'ints from th' reg'lars or anybody else? *I guess not!* No, not by a gol durn sight!"

"You used to put up some pretty stiff work in your line," the colonel hastened to say, after this outburst. "Why, my boys have yelled themselves hoarse many a time when you fellows have gone thundering by to take up position and unlimber."

"Yes, indeed," I put in at this point, "even we *young* men have heard of Burdett's Battery, and the work it did" — which wasn't altogether true, but served to mollify the disturbed sergeant just as well as if it had been.

"Go on, sergeant," said the colonel, "tell us when *you* came in. It isn't possible that you were the — "

"'Twas terrible hot that noon," began the old fellow, as if he had paid no attention to what we had been saying. "Th' air was close an' muggy, an' th' smoke jest hung 'round 's if 'twas too tired t' drift away.

Why, we sent up rings o' smoke from th'
guns that was jes' as perfect 's *that* one,"
pointing towards one I just had blown from
my lips, " an' they lasted a heap sight longer
'n that did, too."

" Yes," assented the colonel, "it certainly
was hotter than — "

" Tophet an' th' brazen hinges thereof,"
said the veteran. " Yes, 'twas *awful* hot, an'
a'ter th' flurry was over — that time we
served th' guns so fast — *I* was jest a-sweat-
in', I kin tell ye. Thirsty, too? Wal, I
ruther *guess!* Prob'bly that was what put
it inter my head t' take a couple o' canteens
an' slip down inter th' medder where your
skirmishers had left their dead an' wounded.
Ye see, a'ter I'd sponged my gun, an' sent
home another shell in case it should be
needed, I took a drink, an' while I had th'
ol' canteen up t' my lips th' thought come
t' me that p'raps some o' th' poor devils
layin' out there in th' sun might be gettin'
dryer 'n all torment."

The colonel had risen from the bench and
slowly was pacing to and fro upon the path,
but he kept his eyes fixed upon the old sergeant, and, when he paused, broke out with,

" So *you* were the one who went to give water
to our boys. Why, man, the risk was awful ! "
" 'Twarn't neither," said the old fellow,
bluntly. " I got back all right, didn't I ? "
and then, as his eye fell upon a long, low
steamer, which was ploughing its way along
towards Newport News, he dismissed the
whole matter with, " B'gosh ! *ain't* that a
pretty sight ? See th' smoke trailin' out
behind, an' watch th' sparkle o' th' water.
Oh, this is a great place in some ways. Here
'tis 'most November, an' I'm settin' out here
'thout no overcoat, an' warm 's a pot o'
beans."

" You were fired upon, weren't you ? "
asked the colonel, whose face wore a look I
never had seen there. Farwell glanced at
the scene before him for a moment longer,
and then turned his eyes upon his questioner.
" Oh, yis, th' Johnnies practised on me a
little, an' I got scratched 'crost th' wrist.
There's th' mark," he said, drawing up his
sleeve, and displaying a scar which ran diagonally across the flesh. " *I* got out of it well
enough, but I was all-fired sorry 'bout that
lieutenant I brought in with me. He was
livin' when I picked him up, but when I

turned him over t' th' boys that run out t' meet me, he was deader 'n a door-nail — shot plum' through th' head while I was a-luggin' him in, *an' I never knowed it!* Must ha' b'en that I was excited — or else my wrist hurt me so I didn't notice. Poor little cuss! I've always felt that he might ha' be'n alive yet 'f I'd let him be. But ye can't tell; no, ye can't tell, an' I *meant* well, anyhow."

" It must be something more than chance that has brought us together," said the colonel. " Why, sergeant, that lieutenant was one of my closest chums — poor little Hale, of Company H. And *you* brought him in ! "

" Wal, I didn't mean t' get him killed," began Farwell, grasping the hand the colonel offered, " an' I'm sorry — "

" You need be sorry for nothing," broke in Colonel Elliott, " for the surgeon looked him over as he lay there in our lines, and found that he had been mortally wounded at first, so the shot that came last was only a merciful one."

" Now, *that's* a piece o' good news," exclaimed the old man. " I've always worried myself, more or less, wonderin' 'f I hadn't oughter ha' let him lay where I found him.

So *'twarn't* my fault? Gosh! I'm glad o'
that! Wal, that's what they give me th'
medal for, an', 's I said in th' fust place, it
don't signify much, one way or t'other."

I got up and shook hands with the old
fellow, and then — because I had a sort of
impression that the colonel would like to be
left for a minute alone with him — I walked
over to the sea-wall, and stood looking out
over the blue waters where the *Cumberland*
had gone down, with the old flag defiantly
waving, and her men still standing by the
smoking guns. But I wasn't thinking of
the heroism that has made this place forever
famous. No; I was wondering if *I* could do
what the old gunner had done, and then
make so little account of it afterwards. I
had been standing there for perhaps ten
minutes, watching the gulls as they lazily
swept by, when I felt a hand upon my
shoulder, and heard the colonel say, "It's
time we were getting back to the hotel.
We've had experiences enough for one morning, eh, Jack? Well, *now* what do you think
of the stuff we had in the old corps?"

"Pretty good stuff, if that's a fair sample,"
I returned, glancing over at the bench where

I had left the old sergeant seated. " Hello! he's gone."

" Yes, there he is, walking back to quarters. But you'll see him again," said the colonel, and as we trudged along back towards the hotel he explained for my approval the details of a scheme which he had evolved.

Well, the upshot of the whole matter was that when we went north, ten days later, Sam — for " Sam " is his official title now — went with us. It took some trouble to get him started, for he had settled himself at Hampton for a winter of ease and genteel laziness. But the colonel has a very persuasive way about him, and finally Sam fell a victim to it. So now he is installed as presiding genius at " The Battery," and under his watchful eye that comfortable roost of ours becomes more comfortable day by day ; for who can build the cheeriest fire, who can most brightly polish our pewter mugs, who can while away a dull half hour with yarns of the by-gone days in camp and field — who, but Sam ?

One drill-night, not long after he had come among us, he turned up at the armory and for nearly an hour stood watching the companies as they went through with their night's work. I noticed him as he stood in one corner of the long hall, and thought that he seemed greatly interested ; but I must admit that I was surprised when, a little later, he walked into the colonel's room and announced that he wished to enlist. Now, the law allows us one orderly at headquarters, and as that place then happened to be unfilled we gave it to him.

The colonel himself mustered him in, and I stood by during the ceremony. Sam stood erect and motionless, and with uplifted hand swore "to bear true faith and allegiance to the Commonwealth of Massachusetts," and after he had slowly repeated the closing words of the military oath — " I do also solemnly swear that I will support the constitution of the United States. *So help me God* " — he let fall his hand, and said, " It's close onto thirty years, Cunnel, sence I said them words, an' th' last time I said 'em they meant a good deal t' me. But they aint lost none o' their meanin' — an' if this reg'ment ever has t' go out *I'll go with it*, though I'd a darn sight ruther be at th' trail of a gun

than go t' foolin' with a muskit at my time
o' life."

Later in the evening I happened to see
Sam's muster rolls lying upon the colonel's
desk, and out of curiosity glanced through
them. " *Name:* Farwell, Samuel," I read,
" *Rank:* Private (Hdq'rs Orderly). *Age:*
65 years. *Occupation:* Gentleman. *Remarks:*
Private, Corporal, Sergeant; Burdett's (N.
H.) Light Battery, U.S. Vols., 1861–65 ;
Medal of Honor for distinguished bravery."
With my finger upon the column in which
Sam's occupation was recorded as that of
" Gentleman," I looked inquiringly at the
colonel, who answered my unspoken question with — " That's right *enough*, Jack.   In
the first place, he's a soldier, and you ought
to know that the profession of the soldier is
the profession of the gentleman.   In the
second place, he wasn't doing anything for
a living when we found him — and   that
surely is gentlemanly.   And lastly, he *is* a
gentleman, every inch of him, and I 'll thank
you not to question it."

OUR HORSE "ACME"

OUR HORSE "ACME."

THE paymaster piled up a neat little heap of documentary odds and ends, shoved it to one side, and banged down upon it a heavy paper-weight. Then he slammed together the thick, leathern covers of the regimental roll-book, and by sheer force of muscle hoisted that precious and ponderous volume up to its appointed resting-place. And finally, after he had sent crashing down the lid of his desk, he thrust his hands into his pockets, drew a long breath, and looked over towards the adjoining desk, where the colonel sat writing.

For a minute or so, after this racket had subsided, the scratching of the colonel's pen steadily continued, but finally there came a long, rasping sound of steel upon paper, denoting the flourish at the end of a signature, and the colonel reached for the blotter, saying, as he applied it to the writing before him, " So you've concluded to call it a day's work, eh? Well, why couldn't you *say* so, instead of making row enough to raise the dead and deafen the living? I take it that your infernal old rolls are straightened out at last."

" Rolls are up to date ; everything's up to date, and I'm square with the game again," replied the paymaster, locking his desk and pocketing the key. "About ready to stroll along, Colonel? Brown has stuck his head in through the doorway a couple of times, with an expression on his face which forces me to think that he considers our room worth more than our company."

" I'm ready to call quits," said the colonel, folding his letter and slipping it into an envelope. "Hello, Brown!" to the armorer, who had made a third suggestive appearance at the door. "Keeping you up? Too bad! Well, you may put out these lights, and in a minute more we'll be out of my room, too. Come along, Pay, it's time decent people were at home."

" But we're not ' decent people,' " objected the paymaster, as he followed the

colonel to his private room beyond ; " we're
officers of the militia, and, in the estimation
of many worthy citizens, that ranks us just
one peg *below* decency. You know Vandercrumb — old Judge Vandercrumb? Well,
t'other day he was at my house and happened to see my commission hanging in the
library. ' What ! ' says he, in a politely disgusted sort of way, ' *you* in the militia?
Well, I must say, Langforth, I'm surprised
to find you guilty of that ! ' " and the paymaster laughed, as he remembered the in-
flection with which the words had been
spoken. The colonel laughed, too, for Langforth had imitated to perfection the tones of
shocked respectability, and the anecdote
amused him the more because it bore so
close a resemblance to many experiences of
his own.

"It always has been so," he said, as he
drew on his light overcoat, " and always will
be, I dare say. People see only one side —
the 'fuss and feather' aspect — of volunteer-
ing, and the traditions of the old ' milishy '
days are slow in dying out. Well, I suppose
we can stand it all, but at times it galls a
bit."

"Yes, it *is* rather rough, to work hard and faithfully, year in and year out, and then be rewarded by hearing some fellow at one's club wondering 'how the devil anybody can take any interest in such boy's play,'" said the paymaster, whose honest love for the service made him peculiarly sensitive to any covert sneers directed at it. "But, as you say, we can stand it; and, besides," he went on, "we have our fun in our quiet way, and I'm weak enough to pity the outsiders, for they miss more downright sport than I would be willing to forego."

"Yes, we certainly have our fun," said Colonel Elliott, as he walked with the paymaster down the granite steps of the armory and out into the deserted street, "but it's been 'all work' to-night, eh, Langforth? Phew! I've written, since eight o'clock, more letters than there are in the whole condemned alphabet."

"I've done my share, too," remarked his companion, taking advantage of the glare of a chance electric light to consult his watch. "Quarter past eleven; well, it might be worse."

"Say, Langforth," observed the colonel,

abruptly halting as they came to a corner,
" if we switch off here and step out a trifle
faster we can flank The Battery, get a pewter and a sandwich, and do it all before midnight.   What do you say — do or don't? "

"Heads, we go ; tails, we also go — home,"
replied Langforth, yawning, and extracting
from his change pocket a nickel.   " *Tails* —
and be hanged to it ! " he ejaculated, as he
held the coin up to the light.   " Well, that
settles it ; we'll go up to The Battery.   It
takes more than a miserable five-cent bit to
send me hungry and thirsty to bed."

" Come ahead, then," said the colonel,
laughing at the ease with which his companion set aside the verdict of the coin.
" That's not such a bad system of yours :
snapping to see what you'll do, and then
doing what you please.   Always work it that
way ? "

"No, not always," returned the paymaster,
lengthening his stride in order to keep up
with the pace set by the colonel, " only
sometimes ; and this is one of the times.
Suppose we shall find anybody up there ? "

" The genial Pollard is sure to be there.
He's a fixture.   Can't see why he pays dues

at his club, can you? Since we started this
institution he's never spent an evening anywhere else. Well, here we are — all except
the stairs," said the colonel, turning in at
the court at whose far end, away up in the
darkness, the lights of The Battery invitingly
twinkled. "Hello!" he exclaimed, a moment
later, as he opened the door at the head of
the last flight of stairs, "here's Pollard, sure
enough — and 'Bones,' and a couple more
men," and with this he walked over towards
the table around which the earlier comers
were seated.

"Colonel Elliott, let me present Lieutenant
Hotchkiss and Ensign Hatch, both of the
Naval Battalion," said the surgeon, rising
and designating these officers with a graceful
wave of his cigar. "Gentlemen, this is
Langforth, our 'Pay.' Ah, you've met
him?" The two late comers drew up chairs,
and made known to Sam their requirements;
and then the colonel, turning towards the
surgeon, said, "Bones, what is it? You look
troubled."

"Well, to tell the truth," replied the
surgeon, ruefully glancing at his questioner,
"I *was* going to tell these fellows how I won

the cavalry cup, but now I suppose I shall have to defer it to another time."

"Oh, go ahead with your yarn — spring it," said the colonel. "'Pay' and I don't mind, and Pollard the genial never will interrupt. Besides, with three of us here, you'll not be apt to deviate very widely from the truth, and truth is desirable in all reports of a military Nature. Go ahead!" and the colonel, with a wink at Langforth, took the mug which Sam had brought him.

"Well, you see, it was like this," began the surgeon, clasping his hands behind his head, and comfortably leaning back in his chair. "In camp, last summer, we had the athletic fever pretty badly, and the way all hands went in for games of various sorts was a caution."

"'Games of various sorts,'" echoed Pollard, winking at the paymaster, and making motions as if dealing a pack of invisible cards. "That's not bad, Bones."

"*Out-door* games of various sorts," amended the surgeon. "Cork up, will you, and don't let these sailors carry away wrong impressions of us."

"All right, old man," replied Pollard,

catching Sam's eye, and holding up one finger to denote drought; "only don't be so ambiguous in your remarks. But really, we did have lots of athletic enthusiasm, last camp, and it was very tiring to see the boys all sweating after some record or other — when they were off duty — instead of lying 'round in their tents and keeping cool."

"The cavalry fellows," resumed Bones, "didn't seem able to muster much talent in the way of track athletes, and for a time they weren't in it at all. But one night, between tattoo and taps, little Whateley — second lieutenant, you know, of 'H' troop — came riding down the lines, stopping at all the regimental headquarters, and finally he brought up at our marquee.

"A few of us were sitting there, smoking a good-night pipe before turning in, and we made him dismount before telling us his errand. Well, I ordered up a little prescription for him, to counteract the effects of the night air, and when he'd got back his breath —"

"Gad!" put in one of the visitors, "is *that* the way your doses work, doctor?"

"Did I say it was the prescription?" inquired the doctor, unclasping his hands, and leaning forward to take a pipe from the table. " He might have been out of breath from riding so far. Anyway, he got his breath back, as I've stated, and used it to remark that the cavalry took a deep interest in military sports, and had chipped in to buy a silver tankard to be ridden for by the mounted officers in the brigade. And he further said — with a grin, too, confound his youthful impudence ! — that he knew we could enter some mighty fine material, for the reputation for horsemanship of our field and staff was more than local.

" Now, that last insinuation was too much, and we told him that he needn't worry— we'd be represented. So off he rode, declining to take another dose of my good medicine, though I told him that the prescription read, ' Repeat as required,' which meant once in five minutes. Well, after he'd gone, we began to talk it all over, and the discussion as to who best could afford to run the risk of breaking his neck for the glory of the regiment and the good of the service was an animated one, you'd do well to believe."

" Yes — and I remember the extreme

modesty with which everybody suggested
some other man for that distinction," remarked the colonel in a reminiscent way,
"and how you all fell over each other in
your anxiety to let somebody else do the
riding and gather in the glory."

"Well, I'd been detailed as Field Officer
of the Day for the date the race was sched-
uled," Major Pollard hastened to explain;
while Langforth promptly came in with the
remark, "And I hardly had got into shape
from my winter's attack of grippe."

"There, *there!*" exclaimed the colonel,
with a wave of his hand, "we don't care to
have all that over again. For my own part,
I couldn't ride because — well, because it
hardly would do for a regimental commander
to so far forget himself as to go in for anything of that sort. See?"

"In other words, six of us didn't dare to
go in, and the remaining half-dozen were
afraid to," said the surgeon, drawing up one
foot to rest it easily across his knee. "Well,
it all ended in my being chosen by acclama-
tion to represent the glorious Third, and,
though I wasn't exactly 'impatient to mount
and ride,' yet I made the best of it, and tried
to pretend that I was."

"It seems to have been acknowledged that you were the best rider in your regiment," suggested one of the visitors.

"Oh, I hardly should care to claim so much as that," replied Bones, with a glance at his brother officers, "but I've been nine years in the service without falling off my horse — and that's a pretty fair record for a staff officer of volunteers. Well, as I've said, I was elected without a dissenting voice — except my own — and the ill-concealed joy of Wilder, our assistant surgeon, was something worth seeing. He's looking for promotion, you know, and a casual broken neck on my part would have given it to him."

"Pardon the interruption," interposed the colonel, blandly, "but there will be a vacancy for Wilder, and very soon, too, if you cast any more reflections upon the horsemanship of my military family."

"Gracious! did I?" asked Bones, hastily. "Impossible! Why, we all ride, and ride well; all except the adjutant. *He can't!*"

"Pardon me again, doctor," said the colonel, sighing wearily, "but the adjutant can ride, too. I've *seen* him."

"If you say so, I suppose I'm not to dispute it," rejoined the surgeon, meekly. "But, if he's such a good rider, don't you think it was just a little rough on him to take him up four flights of stairs, as you did only last week, and introduce him to the wooden vaulting-horse in the regimental gymnasium?" The colonel laughed at this recital of the latest headquarters' joke, and Bones continued, "Well, even if the adjutant *is* rather amateurish in his riding, he at least is entitled to some of the credit for winning the cup, for he furnished my mount.

"You see, Charley had a horse, last camp, that suited him 'way down to the ground. His walking gait was the poetry of motion; in fact, it was hard to get him to move at any faster pace. But somehow, by slapping him with the reins and clucking to him, like a woman calling hens, Charley sometimes managed to get him into a lope that was just about as easy as a rocking-chair, and didn't seem to cover ground much more rapidly than a rocking-chair could. We used to suggest that spurring would be a more military method of getting the beast under way, but Charley always replied that spurs were un-

necessarily cruel things, and that he hadn't
the heart to do anything to interrupt the *en-
tente cordiale* existing between him and his
charger."

" Wasn't it a ratty-looking beast, though ! "
put in Langforth, setting down his mug and
laughing aloud. " We christened him ' Acme, '
he was such a perfect skate. "

" ' Handsome is as handsome does,' " quoted
Bones, sententiously. " His performances were
remarkable, but he *wasn't* much on beauty,
especially at that point of his anatomy where
about a square foot of hide and hair was lacking. However, we got around that blemish
by borrowing some axle grease from one of
the battery drivers and painting the bare
spot so thoroughly that the rest of his hide
looked dingy by contrast.

" Now, ' Acme ' had one little peculiarity
that nobody knew anything about ; nobody,
that is, except Charley and me. You couldn't
touch him with a spur on either flank without making him wheel half 'round to the opposite side and bolt for all that was in him.
It was a pleasant little trick and one that
would throw a man every time unless he knew
what was coming. I know that to be a fact

because, well, because he threw *me* in that way, the very first day we were in camp."

" Thought you'd been nine years in the service without ever being thrown," remarked Hotchkiss, with the air of one scoring a good point.

" Oh! no, I never said that," explained the imperturbable doctor, turning this thrust harmlessly aside. " If you recall my words you will remember that I said I'd never *fallen* off ; to be thrown off is a very different matter."

" Ah ! I see. Pardon my carelessness," said the discomfited naval visitor. " We fellows that go down upon the sea in ships aren't very well up, I fear, in these nice distinctions of the land service."

" Naturally not," said the surgeon, " and of course it's excusable ; but you readily will notice the distinction, which really is as great as that between being in mid-ocean and being ' half-seas over ' would be, in your own case.

" Now, I recalled that little experience of mine with the adjutant's horse, and it occurred to me, when I was casting about for a mount, that if I only could manage to keep

my seat while he was executing his diabolical half-face, I should have a dead cinch on
the cup; for when he *did* run, after one of
those performances, he ran like the very
devil."

"He did, indeed," said the colonel, smiling as if at some remembrance.

"It was on Wednesday night that little
Whateley dropped in on us," Bones continued,
"and the race was on the card for Friday
noon. That was on 'Governor's Day,' you
know, and the camp was sure to be crowded
with visitors. Pleasant outlook for me,
wasn't it?

"Well, on Thursday morning I borrowed
'Acme', and rode a couple of miles out of
camp to a big hay-field I knew of, because I
wished to make sure, by a strictly private
trial, that my little scheme was in reliable
working order. It was. Everything went
to a charm. I got a firm grip on the pommel
and gave 'Acme' the spur; whereupon he
spun half 'round, and was off like a wild en-
gine on a drop grade. Yes, he was off, but,
better still, I was *on*, and when finally I got
him into his rocking-chair lope, I started back
for camp, pretty well satisfied with my

experiment; and all the way along the road
I couldn't help grinning at the thought of the
sensation that was brewing for the next day."

"Well, it *was* a sensation, and that can't
be disputed," commented Pollard, as the
surgeon paused for a moment. "We all
backed you and 'Acme'; not because we
had any particular expectations, but just out
of loyalty to the old regiment, and because
the odds were so inviting. I took ten out of
Mixter, myself."

"Friday morning was cloudy," said the
doctor, after he had brought his pipe to a
satisfactory glow, "and I half hoped that it
would rain before noon, for I was getting the
least shade nervous. Everybody around our
headquarters was so very kind that it made
me fidgety as a school-girl. At breakfast,
in mess, the colonel thoughtfully opened an
elaborate discussion about the proper form of
ceremonies at military burials. The adjutant, on his way to guard mounting, stopped
long enough at my tent to say that ' Acme '
just had killed one of the hostlers, and that
the band had gone out of camp soon after
breakfast for the purpose of practising ' The
Lost Chord.' And *you*, Langforth — con-

found you! I haven't forgotten how you forged my name to an order to have the brigade ambulance report to me at noon, the very hour of the race.

" But somehow the morning went by, and at noon the sky was beautifully clear, though the air was most horribly lifeless and hot. I dressed up in full fig, helmet, sword, and all, according to the conditions, mounted ' Acme,' and rode out upon the parade.

" Pretty nearly the whole brigade had turned out to see the fun, and around the start the crowd was packed closely, while groups of men were scattered here and there along the three furlongs of turf over which the course had been laid out. I had supposed that there would be, at the very least, half-a-dozen entries; but when I had succeeded in manœuvering ' Acme ' through the crowd and up to the line, I found awaiting me just one solitary horseman. It was Porter, captain of " H " troop, and his mount was the same beautiful thoroughbred that he rides from one year's end to the other.

" Wasn't I sick! I never had a patient who felt worse than I did then. But there was no such thing as backing out at that stage of the game, and so I looked as confident as possible, and happier, I hope, than I felt. But when Porter saluted me, with an inquiring sort of glance at my tired-looking mount, and a grin at my audacity in showing up on such a beast, why, I swore under my breath that I'd send the spur into poor old 'Acme' deeply enough to scratch his digestive apparatus."

"It was a funny contrast," laughed Langforth, with his mug in mid-transit from the table to his lips. "Of course, Bones, you're a better looking man, and all that, than Porter; but that horse of his is a perfect picture for style, and when Charley's old skate ambled up beside him we couldn't *help* grinning, any of us. Do you remember, Pollard, how that grease spot on 'Acme's' flank showed up?"

"Do I?" roared the major. "*Don't* I! Why, Bowen, of the brigade-staff, was standing next me, and when he caught sight of that daub of axle-grease he punched me in the ribs and said, 'So you fellows have black-leaded your craft, eh? Now, I call that blasted unsportsmanlike! The other man hasn't worked any funny games like that.'"

" That was all right ! " said the surgeon,
grimly, " I had *my* fun later — after the race
was run.

" We lined up for the start, and it'll be a
long while before I forget the row it raised
when I persisted in planting ' Acme ' at
right angles to the course. Porter got mad,
and announced that he'd come out to race,
and not to take part in a circus. Most of
the brigade set me down for being either
sunstruck or drunk, but I wouldn't budge,
and neither would ' Acme.' Finally Porter
growled out, ' Let's have this nonsense over
with ! It isn't my fault that we can't have
a race. Start us, will you ? ' ' All ready,
major ? ' the starter asked me. ' Confound
it all — yes ! ' said I, looking to see that all
was clear around me, and then getting a
death-grip on the pommel.

" Down went the flag, and off went Porter
at an easy gallop. Up came my spurred
heel, and off went ' Acme,' too, after a whirl-
around that took away the breath of everybody who saw the performance, and knocked
end-ways a couple of gunners who had edged
in too close to the course. Shades of night !
How that old four-legger flew ! I'd rammed

my spur home for business, and the way he
responded beat even my wildest expectations.

"It was the worst run-away ever seen in
camp, and, before I knew it, we'd passed
Porter, passed the finish, passed the last tent
in the long brigade line, and passed the
ditch at the end of the field ; at least, 'Acme'
passed the ditch — *me* they picked out of it."

"It certainly was a remarkable burst of
speed," assented the colonel, laughing until
the tears stood in his eyes. "When we
found that Bones wasn't killed outright, we
went for the cavalry fellows in every way,
shape, and manner that our combined talents
could suggest, and if we failed to make life
a burden to them it wasn't for lack of trying. Come over here," he continued, rising
from his chair, and leading the way to the
opposite side of the room, where, in a double
frame, there hung upon the wall two large
photographs. "These two pictures — which,
by the way, we consider priceless — tell the
whole story. See that one? Well, that's the
enlargement of a snap-shot plate caught by
one of our color-sergeants when Bones was
in full career. Observe the expression of the

face; and, above all, notice that grip on the pommel. Isn't it all grand? Where should Sheridan's ride and Paul Revere's little trip be classed beside *that?* "

" The other picture in the frame," said the doctor, with a pardonable air of pride, " is a photo of the cup itself, and we all think a heap of it. The fellows in the troop, you see, had been going the rounds of the camp, and guying the life out of the Third — and me — for presuming to enter against their crack horse, so the final result was just plain joy for all hands at our headquarters.

" I was excused from parade that after. noon," he continued, knocking the dead ashes from his pipe, " because I was a trifle tired, and more than a trifle sore — in spots. Be- sides, it took one able-bodied darkey the best part of that afternoon to clean the mud off my uniform, knock my helmet out into shape, and straighten out the kinks in my scabbard.

" As for ' Acme ': well, *he* never turned a hair, and after a careless sort of trot around the camp he came back to our stables, look- ing just as unconcerned and sleepy as ever. But he lived high for the rest of that tour of

duty, and nobody seemed to care about referring to him as a 'skate.'"

"'Sporting blood will tell,'" was Hatch's
comment as the doctor led the way to the
chair where the overcoats lay piled. "I
should think, though, that the troopers would
have challenged you to another go."

"They *have* challenged us — and more
than once," said the colonel, as Sam held his
coat for him, "but our invariable reply is
that our surgeon is too precious a bit of bric-
à-brac to risk in any more enterprises of that
sort, and — as none of the rest of us care to
diminish Bones' glory — we have averaged
up matters by keeping the cup and conced-
ing them the championship," and he moved
towards the door; stopping, however, with,
"I wonder which owl this is?" as he caught
the sound of footsteps on the stairs outside.

"Good evening, Colonel," sung out the
new arrival, the adjutant, as he threw wide
the door and stepped blinking into the room.
"Hello, the rest of you! Can't make you
all out, it's so bright here — after the stairs.
What, all going?"

"Yes, it's a good hour beyond taps,"
replied the colonel.

" All right, sir ; I'll go with you, if you'll
wait for me to empty just *one*," said the
adjutant, drawing off his right glove. " It
would be too much to ask me to turn 'round
and go down again without stopping for a
second wind. One up, Sam — right around ;
making six."

" What's new, Charley?" asked the doctor,
as Sam made off towards the base of supplies.

" Can't seem to think of anything," replied
the adjutant, seating himself easily upon the
nearest table, upon which he began vigor-
ously to drum with his knuckles. " Hold on,
though! Now I come to think of it, I saw
' Acme ' to-day. Yes, sir! And he was
drawing a *hearse*, too. *Yes*, sir! I followed
the funeral a block, to make sure. Well,
here's to him!" and the late master of
" Acme " emptied his pewter with one long,
breathless pull, while the doctor slowly
drained *his* mug, saying with unsmiling
solemnity, " To ' Acme.' "

FROM BEYOND THE PYRAMIDS

FROM BEYOND THE PYRAMIDS.

IT was the evening after the battle at Farlow's Farm, and most of us — what's that? You never heard of any such engagement? Now, isn't that odd! Why, it was fought only last year, and for one whole day the papers were full of it. Well, though I had no idea of putting a preface to the story I started to tell, I suppose I must stop long enough to explain why there was a fight, and how it happened that so many of us — all of us, in fact — got back alive from it.

Once a year, you must know, there comes down from the State House, and through "proper channels," a mandate directing each volunteer regiment in the Commonwealth to arm and equip itself, ration and supply itself, and bundle itself out into the country for what officially is known as the Fall Drill. *We* are rather apt to refer to an affair of this sort as "going out with the regiment for the Autumn Manœuvres," because, you see, this sounds more dignified, and lacks the baldness of the official phraseology.

Now, an order for a Fall Drill means *war;* because it entails a long day of marching, a prodigal expenditure of blank cartridges, and, at headquarters, bother and worry beyond reckoning.

Yes, when one of these orders comes down to us we awake to an activity which calls for the largest size of A in the spelling of it. The quartermaster rises to a height of importance hard to estimate, while his sergeant —upon whom devolves the bulk of the work —sinks into a settled gloom of corresponding depth.   The surgeons find themselves pestered with requests to lay in a better brand of liniment than the stuff they took out with them the year before, which, it unanimously is asserted, was too blistering in its effect.   The adjutant grimly sits at his desk and wrestles with the "General Order" until he reaches a state half-way between utter misery and hopeless atheism.   Why? Because he knows to a dead certainty that a copy of it will find its way into every Sunday

paper in town, and therefore tries with might
and main — to say nothing of the aid of the
old order-files for ten years back — to make
of it a lucid and grammatical fragment of
English prose,— an attempt in which he most
signally fails. And the colonel: well, *he* has
the task of tasks, for it becomes his duty and
privilege to evolve the plan of campaign; and
the campaign, mind you, must be one that
can be brought to a successful issue in a
single day. Think of it! Do you suppose
Sherman, or even Grant himself, could have
met without concern such a demand upon
strategic resources?

Days in advance of active operations, the
field officers fill up their cigar-cases and run
out into the country to look over the ground;
constructing, upon their return, amazing
maps, wherein — on generously large sheets
of brown wrapping-paper — a tangle of blue
lines and red ones serves to make plain the
positions for the attack and the defence. Remarkable productions, those maps! — with
long straight marks to indicate the roads, and
zigzag lines to denote fences, and aggregations
of pretzel-like symbols to show where the
woods lie; and many a mystic sign besides to

stand for as many more features in the land-
scape.   Oh, we couldn't do without the
maps, for a campaign that has to be settled
between one sunrise and the next sunset
must be managed very understandingly;
and yet all this doesn't seem to keep the
enlisted man from damning up hill and down
both the maps and their makers when he
finds himself one of a skirmish-line stationed
in what ought to be a dry ditch, but isn't.

Well, last fall we got our annual order,
went through with the usual week's worry
at headquarters, and then railroaded the regiment out to Farlow's Farm for its day of
field work.   The fight was a stubborn one,
and the amount of powder burned was far in
excess of anything before known, for we had
raised a regimental fund and had purchased
with it some odd thousands of cartridges in
addition to the quantity issued by the State.

The tide of battle swept back and forth
until well into the afternoon, but finally the
smoke-cloud lifted — because there were no
more cartridges to be fired away — and in
the lull a flag of truce was sent by the lieutenant-colonel, who humbly begged permission to bury his dead, and also announced his

readiness to accept any decent sort of terms, since the umpires had declared his four companies to have been annihilated. Now, the lieutenant-colonel and his men, you understand, represented the enemy, and since we had been devoting the day to his destruction we sent up a mighty cheer when his submission was made known, voted the whole affair an admirable illustration of grand strategy, and prepared to leave the field to solitude and the sorrowful contemplation of farmer Farlow, its owner.

We formed line, then broke by fours to the right, and started off along the tree-shaded country road. Up at the head of the long column the drums rolled and rattled, while the bugles and fifes joined merrily together in the crazy, rollicking "Wild Irishman" quickstep — an air which never fails to send the Third into its famous, swinging gait. By turning in my saddle, as I rode in my place with the staff, I could see the regiment behind me as it came solidly tramping along — company after company of blue-clad men; rank on rank of snowy helmets; file upon file of sloping rifle-barrels; and midway of all, the colors, rustling their silken folds in

time with the cadenced tread of the men
who bore them.   Far in the rear glowed a
ruddy October sunset, making a fit background for the whole living, moving picture.
It was a stirring sight and a beautiful one,
and I glanced back again and again to see it,
for the picturesque side of the service has a
peculiar charm for me.

" Jove! but that's pretty!" said Van Sickles,
who rode next me on the staff, reining his
horse over a bit closer to mine, and nodding
back towards the following column. " People
sometimes ask me what earthly attraction I
can find in volunteer soldiering. Well, a sight
like *that* certainly has strong attractions for
me," and he gave another long look towards
the rear.

" Yes, this is one of the things outsiders
miss," said I, bringing to bear upon the curb
a light pressure, as I noticed that my horse
gradually was outstepping the others, " and
taking it all together, Van, the outsiders
miss a great deal."

" That's so, Jack," assented Van Sickles,
" but it's hard to make them see it. Time and
again I've tried to explain why I went into
the service, and why I stay in it; but I've

given up that sort of thing now, because my friends only laugh and say, 'Well, you *have* got the fever, Van, but you can't give it to us.'" Here his horse stumbled slightly, but he easily lifted him, and then asked, "Say, old man, who's this Captain Penryhn?" and he waved his hand towards an officer in foreign uniform who was riding next our surgeon.

"Why, you met him," said I, "just before you were sent over to join 'the enemy.'"

"That's true enough; but I barely caught his name, and beyond the fact that he's in British uniform, and that Penryhn is his name and 'captain' his title, I'm still uninformed."

"Well, I can't help you out to any great extent," I rejoined, just as the rattle of the drums gave place to a crash of brazen melody from the band, "for all I know is that he's one of Stearns' acquisitions, is over here on leave, holds his commission in 'Her Majesty's Sixty-fifth,' and seems to be a decent, soldierly sort of fellow. You must remember that I've been more or less on the jump to-day, and haven't had time to cultivate acquaintances."

"We'll get a chance for cultivation later, no doubt," observed Van Sickles as we came in sight of the long train of cars, side-tracked and waiting to take us aboard and carry us back to the city. "He probably will dine with us to-night, and then we can "—

"Battalion — *halt!*" rang out the colonel's voice, and we reined up, as the seven hundred rifles behind us were brought down, with a rattle and crash, to the carry. "Order — *arms!* In place — *rest!*" followed; and we dismounted, and gave over our horses to the men waiting to lead them to their car at the head of the train.

An hour's ride brought us back to the city, a short march through the lamp-lighted streets found us at the great armory, towering up in the dusky twilight, and then, one by one, the companies were dismissed, and seven hundred veterans were set free to resume the pursuits of peace — which I trust they at once did. We of headquarters dined together at the hotel which lies just around the corner, and afterwards, by twos and threes, sauntered up to The Battery, to smoke our after-dinner cigars and fight over again the day's battle.

When Van and I entered the cosey old room the fun had been started. " That's all right about your flank attack," the lieutenant-colonel was saying, in answer to the senior major's assertion that a brilliant move by his detachment had won the day for the attacking side ; " oh, yes — *that's* all right ; but if it had been the ' real thing,' I'd have cut you up into sausage-meat with the sharpshooters I'd tucked into that clump of pines."

" Well, why didn't you — as it was ? " inquired the major, calmly cutting the end from his cigar.

" Because the boys had run short of ammunition," replied the lieutenant-colonel.

" Ah ! they *had*, had they ? " remarked the major sarcastically ; " and if it had been the real old stuff I'd have been wiped out, would I ? Humph ! A bush full of sharpshooters *without ammunition* doesn't seem to strike me as being much of an obstacle. It's no use, Billy — there's where I caught you napping ; empty boxes are empty boxes, whether they've been emptied of blank or ball."

" I was outnumbered, anyway," said the lieutenant-colonel, on the defensive for the second time that day. " How in thunder could I take four companies, and play 'em off against eight?"

"I don't know, I'm sure," pleasantly replied the major. "You thought you could, though, when we planned this thing out. Miscalculated just a hair, eh?"

"Hello, here's Stearns," put in Van, with a view to diverting the conversation into safer courses before the traditional tranquillity of The Battery should become ruffled. "How are you, Tom? Good evening, Captain Penryhn."

Stearns and his companion came up to the fireplace, in which a cheerful blaze had been kindled to take the chill from the air of the cool October evening, and for a moment the discussion was dropped; but it wasn't long before some chance word renewed the argument, and so, on Van's suggestion, we made a change of base to one of the small tables in the corner of the room, and left the strategists to settle their differences without our aid.

Now, it happened that Bones had been called away immediately after dinner, and so Van appropriated the absent surgeon's pet story, and entertained our visitor by telling how the doctor and "Acme" had brought the Cavalry Cup to our headquarters. It happened also that the recital of this yarn of ours reminded the Englishman of an experience of his own — and that was what I had started to tell you when I had to branch off into so many explanations.

"Rather brutal bit of luck, I should call it," observed the English captain, referring to Bones' racing exploit. "Must have been very melancholy for the troopers. Well, luck's a factor that can't be disregarded. I had a rare slice of luck myself, once on a time, and in the way of riding, too. Fancy I'll tell you of it. Do you mind?"

No, we didn't mind; and so Captain Penryhn proceeded to tax our credulity in this wise:

"I ran upon this particular piece of good fortune in — let me think — in '84," said he, bringing out his words slowly and with an accent which fell oddly upon our ears, and yet certainly detracted nothing from the interest of the story. "It was in Egypt, where we'd had to interfere somewhat in the course of matters. Daresay you remember what led up to all the bother?" Van nodded assent, and so I could do no less, though I'm morally certain that our combined knowledge of the Egyptian question could have been put into four lines of type without overcrowding. "Then I'll jump *in medias res* at once," Penryhn went on, "merely stopping to explain how I happened to be in Egypt at that time.

"I then was in the Sixty-fifth— the 'York and Lancaster' regiment —the same corps in which I now hold my captaincy. I was on leave, however, and had obtained permission to attach myself to the staff of Baker Pacha, who was fitting out his expedition for the relief of Tokar. I'd gone into this venture simply for the fun of the thing, but before I got quit of it I was forced to the conclusion that I possibly had been led into it under a mistaken set of impressions; for the fun was much less in quantity and of a far poorer quality than I had anticipated."

Penryhn picked up the mug which Sam had set upon the table, took a long pull at its amber contents, and then remarked, "Do you know, this American beer of yours is very good? In fact, I find myself coming to fancy it strongly, though I must admit that at first I didn't. It's much the same with Americans themselves: we Englishmen really don't care much about them until we learn to know them well, but when we *do* know them we become very fond of them. I found that to be so in the case of Carroll — Major Carroll, of your Eighteenth Regular Cavalry, who was with me on the campaign of which I am telling."

"Of our Eighteenth Cavalry?" said I, inquiringly. "Why, how came he in Egypt?"

"He was looking for sport, as I was," Captain Penryhn replied. "He was military *attaché* at Berlin, and had got leave for a few months. We both were volunteer aides-de-camp to Baker."

Here, noticing that the Englishman had got well towards the last inch of his cigar, I silently proffered my freshly filled case. He half drew out a weed, but pushed it back to its place, saying "I'm of a mind to try one of your pipes, if I may?"

"You certainly shall," said I. "Hi! Sam, bring the cobs." Penryhn took a pipe, filled and lighted it, and then remarked, "Oh, I say! I rather wondered why so many of you were smoking these things, but *now* I don't. Sweet, isn't it, eh?"

"Yes, we call a cobful of plug a comforting sort of smoke," said Van, "and it takes the entire crop of a fifty-acre cornfield to keep The Battery supplied with smoking utensils."

" Not really ? " said our astonished guest.

" Possibly not quite," I put in ; and then, in order to check Van in any further flights of imagination, I asked, " Didn't you have some difficulty, captain, in getting your expedition into shape ? As I recall it, at this late day, Baker Pacha rather came to grief in his attempt at relieving Tokar."

" Difficulty ? " said Penryhn. " Yes, we had an abundance of it. Baker had drawn together a mob of something over five thousand men. Did I say *men?* Sheep would be better — and black sheep, too ; for the rabble we had with us, under the nickname of ' soldiers,' was made up for the most part of cowardly Egyptian *fellahen*, who had been driven into the ranks either through fear of the bastinado or else by the actual application of it Great Wolseley! Never such a mob had masqueraded as an army since war was invented."

" How were you officered ? " asked Stearns, tossing a match to Van, whose pipe had managed to go out.

" Mainly by Egyptians," replied the Englishman, "though there were enough Eu-
ropeans to pound the mass into at least a
semblance of order and discipline. But it's
utterly impossible to put brains into a solid
Egyptian skull, nor can you put any heart
into one of those miserable, half-human *fellahen:* and that was unfortunate, you know,
because it takes a tidy bit of heart to go out
into the desert against the wild tribesmen ;
while as for brains — well, enough brains for
aiming and firing a rifle are almost indis-
pensable. 'Pon my soul, we actually lost
scores of men by the random firing of our
own troops. What d'ye think of *that?* "

"I think you ought to have had Van
Sickles, here, to do a little missionary work
among your marksmen," said I, laughing.
" He's our I.R.P., you know, and since he
came into commission he has been eminently
successful in keeping our boys from killing
each other."

" Beg pardon," said Penrhyn, doubtfully,
" your I.R.P.? "

" Inspector of rifle practice," explained
Van, adding, " Shouldn't think you could
have afforded to waste your darkies in that
fashion."

" My dear fellow," said our visitor, in a tone of the deepest disgust, " it isn't possible to waste an Egyptian soldier. The only waste I can think of is that of the powder and lead it takes to blow him to — to oblivion."

" That was good material to recruit from," remarked Stearns. " Didn't you feel a little shaky about going out with it ? "

" I've not the slightest hesitation in admitting that I did," replied the English captain ; " and just before we started on our final advance, I bet a dinner with Major Carroll that if we got into a fight, our black regiments wouldn't face the music for an hour. It wasn't a bad bet, for I won by a good, wide margin.

" Well, on the fourth of February, in '84, we marched out our 'army' from Trinkitat, waded across the shallow lagoon to the mainland, and struck out over the sands for Tokar — twenty miles away. You think that you have done rapid work to-day in fighting a sham battle inside half-a-dozen hours, but *we* made a record that, in one way, is incomparably better than yours; for we marched four miles, fought just fifteen minutes by

my bracelet watch, and the campaign *ended*
right there! Can you equal that, eh?"

"Blest if it wasn't hustling!" said Stearns.
"You had pretty nearly a soft thing in that
bet of yours, didn't you?"

"It wasn't half a bad speculation," replied
Penryhn, as Sam replaced our empties by
four newly filled pewters. "Bah! a good
part of our fellows couldn't find spirit enough
even to run, and stood stock-still, paralyzed
with fright, until they were cut down in
their tracks. The rest of 'em —and the
braver ones *they* were — set off on a jog-trot
for Trinkitat, going just fast enough to afford
gentle exercise to the cheerful savages, who
trotted along after them and carved them up
at their leisure. Ah, perhaps things weren't
in a devil of a box!"

"I judge that you wasted precious little
time in trying to rally your men," observed
Stearns.

"On that point your judgment is very
fair indeed," returned the Englishman.
"Rallies aren't manufactured out of that
kind of rubbish. I much sooner should
have thought of attempting to catch a hurri-
cane in a scoop-net. Perhaps if I'd been on

hand at the first break I might have had a try or two at it, but it so happened that I'd been sent with a handful of native cavalry to scatter a bunch of horsemen threatening our flank. When I left the column on this errand, Baker was preparing to 'form square,' but the Mahdi's men came dancing in before he had time for the manœuvre, and when we came galloping back from our dash the fight was *over ;* and, as I've said, fifteen minutes had been time, and ample, for the winding up of that campaign.

"It was a very rum go, and I reflected that, under all the circumstances, I might as well devote my time and attention to getting myself, with unpunctured skin, back to Trinkitat. However, I thought I'd edge in a bit towards the flying rabble, on the chance of falling in with Carroll ; and so I spurred into the outskirts of the mob of fright-crazed blacks. As luck would have it, I ran upon my man almost immediately, and to my dying day I never shall forget how he was busying himself.

"You may think it absurd, but when I rode up to your countryman I found him holding by the collar an Egyptian major, whom he was spanking — yes, actually *spanking!* — with the flat of his sword. Affairs were at the last ditch of desperation, and every moment's delay brought death by so much the closer; and yet, for the life of me, I couldn't help laughing at the sight. The poor major was bawling and sobbing with pain and fright, while Carroll was laying it on with jolly goodwill, accompanying each whack with a burst of transatlantic profanity which, under any ordinary circumstances, would have made me shiver.

"But I hadn't any time to waste in watching performances of this sort, and so I rode up closer, yelling, 'Carroll! *Carroll*, old man, are you mad? You've not an instant to spare! The black devils are close upon us! Where's your horse?' Carroll gave two more resounding whacks to his captive, shook him until his teeth rattled, and then set him free, with a parting kick to speed him on his way to safety. Then he looked up at me with, 'Hello, Pen! My horse? That mud-colored major — I hope they'll lift his woolly scalp! — he *shot* my horse! Pulled his revolver, shut both eyes, blazed away, and hit poor old *Selim.*

I swear, Pen, he nearly made me lose my temper!'"

"Were your native officers all as efficient as this one?" I inquired, after we had laughed a little over this piece of marksmanship.

"Why, compared with the others, he was a hero," said Penryhn, in all earnestness, "for he actually fired a shot. Most of 'em turned and ran without even stopping to pull trigger.

"But though all this now may seem funny enough in the telling, the humor of the situation wasn't quite so apparent *then*, for the few seconds that this little occurrence had consumed had brought danger very close to us. The half-naked Arabs had begun to carve their way right into the heart of our stampeding crowd, and from my seat in the saddle I could see them getting altogether too neighborly to suit my ideas of comfort. 'Catch hold of my stirrup,' I said to Carroll, 'and come along out of this.' He sprang towards me, but before he reached my side a great wiry savage came tearing through the mob, and with one sweep of his long sword hamstrung my horse. Probably he meant to have taken a shy next at me, but he lost the chance, for Carroll plumped a bullet into his neck, and he went tumbling down all of a heap. All that, though, was cold comfort; for there we were, *on foot*, and with any odds you please against our getting out of the scrape alive.

" 'The game's up, old fellow,' said I, clearing myself from my struggling horse. 'Come up here to me, and so long as our ammunition lasts we'll fight it out, back to back.' Our chances seemed so desperate, you see, that I didn't give even a thought to escape. 'The hell we will!' responded Carroll, whose language somehow seemed unnecessarily lurid, 'I guess *not!* Pick up your heels, Pen, and make a scramble for it. We can fight just as well running as we can standing still.'

" At the word he started off, and I followed him, for though death seemed inevitable I didn't have quite the courage to stay and face it alone. 'It's no sort of use,' I panted, as we ran along side by side; 'we can't foot it for four miles over this sand — in our boots, too — and get clear of those naked desert-devils.'

" 'Well, who's going to?' was the answer

I got. Carroll had looked over his shoulder, and catching sight of a camel which, urged on by a Soudanese, was lumbering down upon us, he halted and faced about. 'Hi! you black son-of-the-Nile,' he shouted, 'hold up! You *won't?'* he went on, bringing up his revolver, and roaring out his command in Arabic. 'Take that, then!' and he fired twice. The first shot was a clean miss, but at the second the poor chap rolled over and dropped headlong upon the sand, while Carroll jumped to catch the riderless camel. 'Hold him by the nose!' I yelled, 'that's the only way you can manage him!' '*I've* got him,' he sang out in reply, as he caught the dangling cord. 'Whoa! you hump-backed beast of misery! Hi! Steady, you four-legged, graceful nightmare! How in blazes, Pen, can we make him kneel?' "

" Well, how *did* you?" inquired Van, removing his pipe from between his teeth in order to ask the question.

" We simply didn't," said the Englishman, blowing forth a mighty volume of fragrant smoke, and following this up with a succession of short puffs, " because neither of us knew the trick. 'He looks higher than a house,' said

I, as I stood helplessly beside the ungainly animal, 'but we've got to scale him somehow.' 'Here, hold his head,' said Carroll, 'and I'll make a bluff at mounting him,' and then, after we had exchanged places, he sprang up, caught at some part or other of the camel's trappings, and managed to haul himself up. 'Pass up the lines, Pen, and look lively,' he called out. 'Old Humpty's getting uneasy — and so am I. Give me your hand, and climb as if the Mahdi himself were after you!' I tossed him the rein, and started to follow him up, but the minute I released the camel's head the terrified beast lunged forward, knocking me over like a ninepin, and when I got to my feet again he was fifty yards away — and going like a race-horse.

" ' Clean bowled!' I muttered, as I realized what had happened. 'He can't manage him, so my last chance is played,' and with a farewell glance at Carroll's receding figure I faced towards the desert — the direction from which I knew my death was on its way to me — drew my revolver, filled an empty chamber in it, cocked it, and waited for the end.

" All around me the rush of terror-stricken

blacks continued, while in front, and not far
away, I could catch the flash and gleam of steel
when some Arab butcher hove his sword up
into the air, to bring it whistling down upon
one of our defenceless darkies. Frightened?
Yes, I was in a blue funk, but it was the
sort of fear that has a good share of ugliness
in it, and I shut my teeth down and watched
out for some one to kill.

"In a fix like that a little time goes a long
way, and it seemed as though I had been
standing there for hours — though probably
it was a matter of but minutes — when a
long, misshapen shadow darkened the sand
beside me, and I heard a voice shouting,
'Quick, Pen, for your life! Your hand, old
chap — *your hand!* I can't control this
fellow much longer!' It was Carroll — the
blessed, profane old angel! — who had worked
some Yankee miracle with that camel, and
had come back to pick me out of the wreck.

"Without a word, for seconds were precious then, I thrust my revolver into my belt
— not the most careful thing I could have
done, considering that it was full-cocked —
and by a desperate bit of scrambling got up
behind my rescuer. Off started the camel,

stretched out at top-speed, swaying from side to side, and plunging and rising like a troop-ship in the Bay of Biscay, while we two fugitives clung to whatever we could lay hands upon. But it was comforting to note the rate at which he took himself over the sand, and I actually began to pluck up a trifle."

"Then you didn't complain of your accommodations," remarked Stearns, suggestively.

"I? No, I wouldn't have minded being tossed in a blanket if each toss had sent me away from Osman Digna's sweating savages.

"Well, we hung on like monkeys, and after a time became used to the jolting. Finally Carroll turned his head and said, 'You all right, Pen?'

"'Yes; and you?' said I.

"'Happy as a hoo-poo,' said he; 'but I've got all I can do to steer. You'll have to do the shooting, old man; and when your gun goes dry you'll find two shots left in mine. Help yourself to it, if you need it.'

"Now, I'm quite certain that I couldn't have hit a bungalow, under the circumstances, but I piped up cheerfully with, 'All right;

you keep your eye out for Trinkitat, and I'll
'tend to matters at this end.'

"Luckily I didn't have to experiment at
holding on with one hand and shooting with
the other, for our long-legged mount held his
gait nobly, and took us into Trinkitat, sound
and safe, and at such a rate of going that we
weren't much behind Baker and those of his
staff who had escaped with him."

"Hm! that was a near call, Captain Penryhn," observed Van Sickles.

"I certainly thought so at the time," said
the Englishman, shifting his position in his
chair, "and I've seen no cause since to
change my opinion. Carroll affected to
make light of the whole affair, though, and
declared that we could have got away on
foot; and to prove it, he brought up the
case of his Egyptian major, who actually
managed to escape."

"No! Really?" asked Stearns. "I should
hope that he and Carroll didn't meet afterwards."

"But they did," said Penryhn, with an
expansive grin. "Oh, yes, they met — and
it was a funny meeting, too. Carroll walked
right up to his man, grabbed him by the

hand, and congratulated him on his escape.
And then he apologized for his conduct, and
said that he felt compelled to give satisfaction
for it; wherefore he would meet the ag-
grieved Egyptian whenever and wherever he
might choose, and would fight him in whatever way he might be pleased to suggest.
But this generous offer was too much for our
native friend, and with a profusion of thanks
truly Oriental he declined it, even going so
far as to declare that the slapping he had
undergone at the hands of the ever-noble
and beneficent Carroll — 'might his illus-
trious line long be permitted to continue!'
— without doubt had saved his life, since it
had been the means of spurring him on to a
magnificent and gloriously maintained dash
for safety. And so that matter ended hap-
pily and to the complete satisfaction of all
concerned."

At this point the colonel came over to our
corner and carried away Penryhn to show
him the photographs of our field-work of the
previous year. Stearns got up and went
with them, leaving Van and me to smoke in
comfort and exchange at our leisure our
views of things in general. Now, that man

Van Sickles is a sceptical sort of person, and he began to question the probability of the Englishman's story; but I maintained, as I still do, that it must have been true — for I'm myself something of a liar, and it's hard work for a brother-prevaricator to take me into camp. So I tell you the yarn in the full confidence that it is a true one; and I further will remark that last spring Penryhn sent over to Stearns an Arab shield, together with half a dozen villainous, iron-bound spears and a couple of long, straight, nasty-looking swords, all of which things now may be seen up in The Battery, where we've arranged them upon the wall, above the big book-case.

THE HYMN THAT HELPED

THE HYMN THAT HELPED.

IT was a warm night, late in May. For
two long hours the battalion steadily
had kept at it — ploying into column,
deploying again into line, and varying things
by an occasional march, in company front,
around the great hall. But there comes an
end to all things, even to a two hours' tramp
over an unyielding floor, and at last the
bugler, standing beneath the crowded specta-
tors' gallery, puckered his lips, puffed out his
cheeks, and blew the welcome bars of " Recall " — the signal that it was ten o'clock and
time to wind up the evening's drill. One by
one the companies filed out through the broad
doorway, and as the last man passed over the
threshold — even while the closing notes of
the bugle-call still faintly rang among the
arching trusses of the vaulted roof — the
waiting armorer pressed down the lever
which, at a single touch, extinguished the

lights in the double row of chandeliers, and left the drill-hall to silence and darkness.

But if all was dark and still in the hall below, upstairs the state of affairs was in lively contrast, for in the company quarters there was light in plenty and the hum of many voices, while presently a yell of laughter from " K's " rooms, followed by a responsive roar from " A's " corner, across the corridor, seemed to show that the manœuvres of the evening had not brought the men to the point of complete exhaustion.

About the adjutant's desk, in the staff-room, a knot of officers had gathered to talk over the night's work, and speculate upon the weather of the morrow, for it was the night before Memorial Day, and the four companies detailed for escort duty in the coming parade had been going through a battalion drill, " To get shaken into shape for exhibition purposes," as the major put it.

" The boys measured off a good step tonight: thirty elegant inches, within an eighth," said the adjutant, footing up the last column of the drill report, and then gracing it with his undecipherable signature. " Yes, they stretched it out in gorgeous style,

and the last time they came 'round the hall
the company wheels were just as pretty as
any you ever saw on a little, red wagon."
This was in the days when Upton yet was
law in the land; before the "new regula-
tions" had come to vex the souls of company
commanders.

"That's all well enough," remarked the
major who was to command the battalion
next day; "but, after all, we're at the mercy
of whatever band we catch. It was a mistake
to let ours go out of town for to-morrow."

"It *was* so," assented the adjutant, shoving
a handful of documents into the pigeon-hole
labelled "Papers awaiting action," and then,
rising from his desk, "Do you know what
band's been assigned?"

"Haven't heard," replied the major, with a
yawn. "*I* wouldn't ask for any better marching music than the article the drum-corps
deals out. The boys swing along like ma-
chines, when they have the old tunes to set
'em going;" and he began to whistle "The
British Grenadier," drumming with his fingers an accompaniment to the inspiring, old
refrain, but stopping when the sergeant-major
entered and said, "The colonel presents his

compliments, and wishes the field and staff to report to him in his room."

"Come along, fellows," said the major, buttoning up his fatigue jacket. "This means an expedition against The Battery," and with this safe prediction he led the way along the corridor towards the door which bore upon its oaken panel the words "Colonel, Third Infantry."

"Come in," sang out the colonel, as the group of officers reached his door, "come in for a minute. I need your advice. Only *four* of you? Why, where's 'Pay'?"

The major replied, "He's escaped, sir, but those of us who are left are very much at your service — and full of advice."

"No doubt of it," laughed the colonel; "I've not the slightest doubt of it. That's where the officer of volunteers never is found lacking. I've yet to meet the one who's not prepared to give advice on any matter, and at a minute's notice, too. Well, now for that same advice : do you counsel an immediate and early scattering, or a brief visit to the dominions of Sam ? Weigh your words, for I've determined to be guided to-night by the wishes of the majority."

"I haven't attained a 'majority'—as yet,
sir," said the adjutant, speaking rapidly and
beginning to unbuckle his belt; "but with due
deference to my seniors, I would state that
the evening has been long, warm, and very
arid; enough so to reduce some of us — *one*
I can swear to — to a state bordering upon
collapse. I therefore most respectfully would
suggest that The Battery be converted tem-
porarily into a field-hospital, and that Major
Sawin, surgeon, Third Infantry, be ordered
to proceed thither without delay, to make
provision for such patients as later may
report to him for treatment."

"Listen to the boy!" said the colonel, as
the adjutant paused for lack of breath.
"And nobody has any better advice to
offer?" he went on. "Well, Bones, you
heard? Trot along—you're not in uniform
—and start Sam on a bowl of claret-cup.
The rest of us will join you in ten minutes."

"I think *I'll* do the compounding," said
the surgeon, mentally recalling a formula of
his earlier days, "and if the results aren't
satisfactory — why, I'll resign and give Wilder his step;" and he turned towards the
door, pausing to remark, "Don't overheat

yourselves by hurrying, for I'm going to take my time in getting there."

The ten minutes had stretched well along towards twenty, when an uneven trampling of feet upon The Battery's stairs warned the waiting surgeon that his patients were at hand. He had employed his time to good purpose, however, and in the arrangement of his " field-hospital " there lacked nothing which long experience could suggest.

Before the wide dormer-window — in which every sash had been thrown open to catch whatever of breeze might stray that way — stood a round table, bearing a huge glass pitcher, filled to the brim with crimson claret-cup, and beaded with the dew of its icy contents. Five heavy chairs were ranged near at hand, and to each a glass was allotted, while beside every glass lay a newly filled pipe, ready for the lighting. Save one shaded lamp, all the lights were out, to give full play to the bright moonlight which came slanting in through the casement, tracing curious patterns of light and shadow upon the floor and walls. All looked cool and restful, and the surgeon gave just one more satisfied glance at his preparations before turning to receive his wearied brothers-in-arms.

"This way to the operating-table," he called out, as the door was flung open. "The instruments are ready, and the surgeon is waiting. I shall make no diagnosis in individual cases — since it is apparent that your ailment has reached the proportions of an epidemic — but shall treat you collectively."

"Bones, you deserve to be thanked 'in orders,'" said the colonel impressively, after a comprehensive survey of the surroundings. "Sit down, all — and Charley, you man the pitcher."

"I chose a pitcher in preference to a bowl," explained the beaming doctor, waving his hand in the direction of that seductive-looking vessel, "because the effect upon the eye is so much more pleasing. I tell you, the careful practitioner has to watch out for even the most trifling details."

A clatter of chairs followed this remark, succeeded by the musical tinkle of ice, as the adjutant filled the glasses. Then came a moment of refreshing silence; and finally five grateful men set down their empty tumblers with a universal, long-drawn sigh of comfort and supreme content.

" Wilder will not get his step *this* time," said the colonel, holding his glass in readiness for refilling, " for your reputation, Bones, is saved."

" Your appreciation touches me," replied the surgeon, leaning forward to possess himself of a pipe, an example followed by the others.   One after another the matches cracked and flamed, until five corn-cobs glowed soothingly in the dim, half-light of the quiet room, sending a pale cloud of fragrant smoke adrift across the moonbeams, to twist and circle in the fitful current of air from the open casement.

" With the brigade band, which you'll have to-morrow," observed the colonel, between puffs, to the major, " you ought to go ' swinging on the old, old gait.' "

" So it's to be the brigade band ? " said the major.   " Good enough !   Just before we left the armory we were discussing our chances on music."

" Well, music is rather important," returned the colonel, " for a good band can put life into the lamest column.   I once even knew a band to put life into a dead man, too. Fact!"

"Extraordinary!" murmured the major. "I've heard plenty of bands bad enough to strike a man dead, but I never happened to discover one that seemed quite up to the resurrection pitch. Perhaps, Colonel, you'll tell us about it?"

"I'm blessed if I don't," was the colonel's reply to this suggestion, "if for nothing else than punishment for the doubt implied in your tone."

"Thank you, sir," said the major politely, bestowing his lazy length upon the cushions of the window-seat, where he settled himself in all comfort. "It's a good long time since we've had a yarn from you, and I'm pleased to learn that we're in a fair way to get you started."

This judicious remark was not without its effect, for the chief pulled the major's empty chair handily near, gently deposited his feet upon it, and observed, "Well, if I've told you this incident at all, I'm sure it hasn't been within a year, so it will be as good as new." Then he turned his head and called, "Sam, come and put out that lamp," adding,

"Moonlight's good enough for story-telling — and somehow lamplight makes a discord on a night like this."

" Got ev'rythin' handy, Cun'l?" inquired Sam, as the flame flickered and went out.

" Yes, everything except *you*," responded the commanding officer. " Pull up a chair, Sam, and kindle your disreputable old briar-wood; for I'm going to yarn about a shindy in which your battery trumped the winning trick, and I shall need your corroborative testimony."

Sam brought a chair, seated himself with proper deliberation, and added his contribution to the ever-thickening cloud of smoke; those whose glasses stood in need of refilling took the precautions necessary to avert a drought; and the colonel, fixing his eyes upon the cloudless sky without, began :

" Back in '64 — a matter of a fortnight or so before that little affair at Three Mile Creek, where you, Sam, got scraped across the wrist, and won that medal of yours — the 'Old Regiment' found itself at a most forsaken sort of place which was going to ruin under the name of Ashford Four Corners. Why we had been dumped down in

that particular spot we neither knew nor
greatly cared, for we had reached a point
in soldierly indifference which enabled us
to take our billet unquestioningly, though
not always uncomplainingly. Even old
Burleigh, our colonel, hadn't a very definite
conception of our exact errand, for he told
us that we had been ordered to sit down,
keep our eyes open, and stay there until
we were sent for, — an order which, at the
time, seemed easy of execution, though
rather purposeless.

" With all due pomp and circumstance we
marched into and through Ashford Four
Corners, and took up a position about half
a mile beyond the straggling collection of
tumble-down buildings composing that
metropolis; and there we prepared to ' sit
down,' as *per* orders, and ' keep our eyes
open ' to see that nothing came along over
a sandy road running off, in a southeasterly
direction, into the dense woods in our front."

" Wal, 'twarnt sich a bad idee, havin' ye
thar," observed Sam, between puffs, " an' I
guess ye seen th' reason for't, finally."

" Oh, yes, the reason made itself un-
pleasantly obvious later," assented the col-

onel; " but along at the first we were rather
pleased at being sent off and — as we thought
— side-tracked, for we hadn't the slightest
expectation of seeing or hearing anything
from the enemy. No, we certainly weren't
grumbling much over the detail, for we'd
had a hot and trying time of it for ten days
hand-running, and the prospect of even a
few hours of rest and quiet seemed at-
tractive.

"But though we weren't looking for
trouble, we'd ' been in the business ' too
long to take anything for granted, and so
we had a turn at pick-and-shovel drill, and
threw up a very workmanlike line of breastworks, neatly topped off with logs; and after
the earth had been heaped up and patted
down we surveyed the result of our labors,
called it good, and waited patiently to see if
anybody would blunder along that way to
help us in a house-warming.

"In billiards ' position is everything,' " the
colonel observed, after a short pause to obtain necessary restoratives, "and the same
rule applies in war. Our position, as we lay
at ease in our hastily constructed works, was
fairly good. If I had the blackboard here

I could show you, in ten strokes of the chalk, just how the land lay; but the blackboard isn't here, and, moreover, I should be too lazy to lift the chalk if it *were* here; and therefore I'll state that our line was established across the tapering end of a fan-shaped clearing, and in such a manner that both flanks were protected by dense woods, while on our left an impenetrable swamp afforded us additional security. The open ground in our front stretched away for a distance of about five hundred yards, ending at the edge of the unbroken forest. Do I make clear the situation?"

" Perfectly, sir," said the adjutant, rattling the ice in the pitcher, by way of serving notice that he stood ready to fill any or all depleted glasses.

"'Twas a good 'nough lay-out for in- f'ntry," commented Sam, "but thar warn't quite th' right slope t' git th' best work out o' guns."

" I daresay not," said the colonel, in reply to this bit of criticism, "but your guns were able to accomplish all that we asked, eh? By the way, did you *ever* get a position that suited your exacting taste?"

"Wal, yis," remarked Sam, after an instant of meditation, "seems like we *did* once — at Malvern Hill. We hed jest th' right drop, thar, an' our plungin' fire cut out work thet warn't far from bein' plain butchery."

"After we'd got settled," resumed the colonel, "we began to look about for amusement; but the 'Four Corners' didn't seem to afford much in that line, and so most of us put in our time at making up lost sleep, and we certainly might have found less profitable employment. Of course we sent out foraging parties, but the few unhappy hens that fell into their hands didn't go far towards making chicken salad for four hundred hungry men, and so we fell back upon our usual healthful diet of hard-tack and 'salt horse.' Lord! what wouldn't I have given for a bottle of cold beer, or a pitcher of this blessed mixture," and the chief, moved by the recollection of past privations, emptied his half-filled glass at a single swallow.

The watchful adjutant promptly made good the deficiency in his superior's tumbler, and then did himself a like kindness; Van Sickles, who quietly had been smoking in a shadowy corner, rose, stretched himself, and flung himself down upon the end of the window-seat opposite the major; and then the colonel — just as the city clocks began to strike eleven — went on, " Up to nightfall there had been no developments, and when we bundled ourselves up in our blankets, after posting pickets, it was with a comfortable feeling that we were in for a quiet night.

" I'd been officer of the guard the night before, and probably I don't need to say how soundly I fell asleep. But when, along towards morning, a shot rang out from somewhere in the darkness beyond, followed by another, and then by two or three in quick succession — why, I came rolling out of my blankets in almighty short order, and it didn't take an alarm-clock to tell me that it was time to be getting up. Well, the long roll sounded, the regiment fell in, and presently in came the pickets to report the enemy in our front.

" By this time the night was pretty well along, and the first hazy light of the new day was beginning to come; but there wasn't quite enough of it to show us what was going on across the clearing, and so we threw out skirmishers into the woods on either flank, and waited for the next number on the programme. For a good half-hour we stood there, behind the breastworks, without being able to detect a movement in our front; and I — believing the whole thing due to an attack of 'nerves' — had begun to try what satisfaction I could get from damning the eyes and ears of the pickets who had spoiled my beauty-sleep, when Bob Sheldon, my captain, touched my arm, and silently pointed out towards the clearing.

"Now, all this time the light had been gathering strength, and though it still was too dim to enable us easily to distinguish objects at any distance, I yet could make out what seemed to be a line of skirmishers, slowly moving up towards us. A second glance told me that my eyes had not deceived me, and I turned towards Sheldon, with, 'My apologies to the pickets. I damned 'em too hastily, for we're to have company at breakfast, surer than gospel.' 'Yes; them's them,' said Bob, 'but not all of 'em. I'd give a pipeful of plug to know what's hidden over there in the woods.' 'Where'd be the fun in that?' I inquired, stooping over to rub

my knee, which had stiffened up a trifle
during the night. 'If we knew what was
coming, the chances are that we'd leg it;
and then what would become of the reputa-
tions we've been so long in building up?'

"I straightened up, as I spoke, and again
peered over the crest of the breastwork, dis-
covering that the advancing line had halted
about two hundred yards from us, evidently
without any great ambition to attempt a
closer investigation; for at this stage in the
war, you must understand, both the Confederates and we had learned to think twice
before intruding upon a force well entrenched.
These fellows, however, didn't get much time
to ponder on the situation, for we gave them
a volley which sent them to the rear again,
though they retired slowly, and fired as they
fell back."

"About as my skirmishers did last October," said the major, half to himself, as he
recalled an episode of the regiment's latest
engagement.

"Yes; exactly as your men did," said
the chief, catching this remark, "with this
exception: your boys *all* went back, but
when this line gave ground it left three poor

devils lying motionless in the damp grass. Ah, yes; a 'Fall Drill' would be very like a real fight — if it weren't so different," and he paused to liven up his pipe by a few quick, strong puffs.

"This little exchange of compliments — the way we had in those days, you know, of saying 'How d'ye do?' — was only the curtain-raiser to the real performance," the colonel resumed, after his pipe again had begun to glow and smoke like a toy volcano, "and we hadn't long to wait for the beginning of it. In something less than fifteen minutes after we'd cut loose with that preliminary volley, a regiment came marching out from the woods, changed direction to the right, and formed line of battle; another followed it, and formed on its left; and in the interval between them a battery swung into position and unlimbered. That made the odds two to one, in infantry — and six to nothing in the matter of guns."

"Then ye don't count th' breastworks for nothin'?" queried Sam, who was in a critical mood.

"Well, they ought to be considered," admitted the colonel, with a laugh, "and I'll

call it an even thing on infantry, but the
guns we'll have to figure at sixes and zeros;
and as an old gunner, Sam, you'll admit
that the other fellows held the stronger hand.

"Now, we didn't care much for the infantry part of the show, but the artillery
feature promised to be interesting. The
sight of those six guns, I make no bones of
admitting, worried me considerably; and
even old Burleigh himself showed signs of
unusual animation when he turned to Frazier,
our quartermaster, with, 'Frazier, did you
ever see a man ride like hell?' 'Yes, sir,
I've seen several men riding that way,'
replied the quartermaster. 'Well, then,'
blurted out old Burleigh, 'get on your horse,
and ride back to the brigade — in *just* that
way! Give the general my compliments, and
tell him I want some guns, and in the biggest
kind of hurry, too, if I'm to hold this position. Say that I've got a brigade, at the
least, to handle, and nobody knows how
much more. I guess I can stand 'em off for
an hour, unless they're in force enough to
walk right over me, and I'll give you exactly
those sixty minutes for getting the guns
here. That's all — go! and Frazier started

at a gallop, just as the first shell came screeching across the clearing.

" 'Twas all-fired short range for artill'ry work," commented Sam, at this point, "an' I've always allowed thet th' only thing thet saved ye were raw gunners. *Must* ha' be'n that, for guns half handled would ha' had ye dead an' buried 'fore we got up."

"Yes, the guns seemed frightfully near," assented the chief, slightly shifting his position, to bring his glass within easier reach, "and I think your guess about the gunners must be a good one, for a smartly handled battery ought to have wiped us off the face of the earth in less than half the time that we faced this one. In fact, now that I come to think of it, I remember noticing that most of the shells went over us, and wondering how soon the pieces would be depressed sufficiently to knock our line of works into a cocked hat.

"Well, as I've said, Frazier left for the rear in something of a hurry, and none of us devoted much time to watching his departure, for in front there was more than plenty to take up our attention. Five hundred yards was as long range for the muskets of those days as it was close quarters for guns; but we couldn't stand idle and take *all* the pounding, and so we went in for a little firing on our own account.

" For a time things were rather in a mixed-up mess, and I had my hands full in seeing that my boys kept cool — or decently near it — and didn't go to chucking their ammunition away too generously; so you can understand that I had no eye for anything except what went on in my immediate vicinity. But I can remember, as distinctly as if it had occurred but yesterday, how I turned, when a shell burst just over us, and saw poor Bob Sheldon throw up his hands, stagger, and go plunging down, flat upon his face. I was at his side in an instant, but there was nothing to be done, for he lay there *dead*, with the blood gushing in torrents from a frightful wound which apparently had crushed in his skull. Poor old Bob! I turned him over upon his back, gave just one hurried look at him, and then went back to the company, for — our second lieutenant being then in hospital — I was the only officer left."

The colonel paused long enough to take a sip from his glass, holding it for an instant

up before him to catch the effect of the
bright moonlight upon the ruddy claret.
Then he went on: "Just how long we'd
been at it I'm not certain — for it's hard to
compute time when every minute is crowded
with noise, and smoke, and death; but
finally there came a let-up in the firing, and
with it an indescribable sort of feeling that
something new was about to happen. I was
walking up and down behind my company —
now and again saying a word to steady the
boys — when, from our rear, I heard the
music of a military band; and presently, as
it drew nearer, I caught the air it was playing. It was our own band — we were one
of the few volunteer regiments provided with
such a luxury — and old Colonel Burleigh
had ordered it to march up to the front,
playing for all it was worth, in the hope that
the Confederates might be led to believe that
we were being reënforced.

"Now, we were a careless and godless set,
the most of us, but we were a Massachusetts
regiment, New Englanders born and bred,
and we all knew the 'psalm tunes' of our
boyhood days; so when the band came
marching up, thundering out the 'Portu

guese Hymn ' — that grand old psalm beginning,

' How firm a foundation, ye saints of the Lord,' —

the effect was instantaneous. The old colonel
afterwards told us that he had intended to
pass along word for the boys to set up a
cheer when the band began to play, but the
command never was given ; for when our
fellows recognized the old, familiar air, they
rose as one man, and shouted and yelled, and
yelled again, until the woods reëchoed with
the cheering.

" The cheering was at its height when an
inspiration came to our color-sergeant — a
great, bearded fellow, with a voice like a
trumpet — and, holding high in air the torn
and faded colors, he sprang upon the breastworks, and roared out the second verse of
the hymn —

' Fear not, I am with thee ; oh, be not dismayed !
I, I am thy God, and will still give thee aid ;
I'll strengthen thee, help thee, and cause thee to stand,
Upheld by my righteous, omnipotent hand.'

"It was magnificent ! One after another
the boys joined in the refrain, until four hun-

dred throats swelled the chorus, and four
hundred strong voices sang the old psalm as
it never had been sung before. It was one
of those moments that make an impression
upon the memory which only death can
efface, and I never shall forget the electric
thrill which ran along our worn-out line as
we sung those words of mighty comfort and
cheer.

"I had joined in with the rest, and was
singing for all that was in me, when I heard
at my side a weak voice trying to follow the
air, and, looking down, I saw Bob Sheldon —
whom I had thought dead — supporting himself on one elbow, and feebly wandering
along upon the words of the hymn. It was
a ghastly sight, for he was covered with blood
from the gaping wound in his head, and so
begrimed with the dirt which had clung to
it that his own mother never could have
recognized him. He was alive, to be sure,
but barely alive; and as I knelt beside him
he sank back with a pitifully feeble groan,
for the effort he had made had exhausted
the little strength that was left in him.

"Supporting his head with one arm, I
moistened his lips from my canteen, and then

bent over to catch what he was saying; for,
though his eyes were closed, he was muttering indistinctly, and I could make out an
occasional word or short sentence. 'Nell —
little Nell,' I heard him murmur, 'it's *hard*
to go away.' Poor old Bob! I knew in a
minute that he was clean out of his head,
and that his thoughts had gone wandering
back to his old New England town, and to
the brown-haired girl who, with brimming
eyes and quivering lips, had bidden him God-
speed when the 'Old Regiment' marched
away. 'Be patient and — and brave, dear,'
he rambled on, in his feeble voice, 'for I'm
surely, surely coming — back — to you.'
Was he? Gad! something caught me in the
throat when I heard the words," and the
colonel abruptly paused, and reached for his
glass.

Half unconsciously the major slipped his
hand inside the breast of his coat, where it
rested upon a much-worn leathern case in
which lay hidden a photograph; the adjutant
blew a succession of feathery smoke-rings
across the broad beam of moonlight which
came streaming into the room, and — for he
was a very young man — fancied that each

ring framed a certain sunny face; Van
Sickles tranquilly went on with his pipe;
and the colonel, clearing his throat by a
slight cough, continued:

"Now, all this meant a great deal to me,
for I had known from childhood both Sheldon and the girl whom he was to marry.
And I can remember how I wondered, as I
knelt there, if it would be my duty to tell
her how her lover had gone down at his post.
I tell you, boys," and his teeth tightened a
bit upon the reed stem of his pipe, "war has
a terrible fascination — I wouldn't willingly
wipe away the memory of the old days in the
service — and yet many an experience of
mine made me stop to think if, after all, war
were worth the while.

"But in this case matters turned out all
right in the end," went on the chief, reaching
for the jar of tobacco, and extracting a pipeful, which he slowly rubbed in the palm
of one hand, "and when the 'Old Regiment'
marched through the crowded streets of
Washington, in the grand review. Bob Sheldon rode along with us — and his straps bore
the gold leaves, in place of the silver bars.
Yes, he pulled through all right, and not long

after we were mustered out, I stood with him in the little church at home, and saw his handsome face light up when Nell — his 'little Nell' — came blushing down the aisle to end the long waiting.

"You see, the flying splinter of shell that had crushed him down had torn a frightful furrow in his scalp, and had stunned him for a time; but the skull wasn't fractured, and so, after a few weeks, he came back from hospital to us, strong and hearty, and nearly as handsome as ever. And now, Ned," glancing towards the major, and holding a flaming match above his freshly filled cob-pipe, "I've demonstrated to you how a band — if it's a good one and judicious in the selection of its music — can call a dead man back to life."

"But the fight, sir?" asked Van Sickles, from his lounging-place upon the cushions; "how did the fight come out?"

"Why, that's so! I forgot to mention how the affair ended," said the colonel, rising with a yawn. "Sam, you tell 'em; you know as much as I do about the rest of it."

"Wal, I dunno's thar's much more t' tell," drawled the old gunner, in response to this

command. "Fact is, thar warn't much
fightin' a'ter th' reg'ment'd got through
with its praise-meetin'. Ye see, soon's th' ol'
gineral heard th' sound o' th' guns down
Ashford way, he started a couple o' troops
an' our batt'ry a-jumpin', an' we met Cun'l
Burleigh's messenger on th' road. Wal, we
sweat our teams some, an' got down thar real
suddin ; an' 'fore we'd done enough firin' t'
heat th' guns, th' rebs pulled out o' th' clear-
in', hoss, foot, an' artill'ry — only thar
warn't no hoss — an' took 'emselves off out
o' th' way."

"Yes, that was the way it ended," said the
chief, as Sam closed his official report of the
action. "And now we must be getting along
towards bed. Don't set too stiff a pace for
us, Ned, in the parade ; for all of the old boys
aren't so able-bodied as I am, and to-morrow
there'll be many a man in the Grand Army
who'll have a hard struggle between pride
and stiffened joints. Wonder why I lighted
this pipe ! Well, it's late, and I'm going
to risk being caught on the street with it.
Good-night, Sam."

"What's become of your man Sheldon,
since the war ? " asked Van Sickles, as

the little party picked its way down the stairs.

"I've lost him," replied the colonel, in an altered tone. "It's a long story, Van, and a sad one. Some other time, perhaps, I'll tell you; but not now."

THE SEVENTH MAJOR

THE SEVENTH MAJOR.

"I WAS a-tryin'," Sam once meditatively remarked, up in The Battery, as he straightened himself up after carefully depositing a fresh log upon the blazing fire, — "I was a-tryin' t' figger out how many majors we've got now. Startin' at th' top, thar's three *real* majors, which are three; then thar be th' surg'n — he bein' also a major likewise — comin' t' four; then th' sargint-major an' drum-major totals her up t' six — an' then in comes Major Larry Callahan, at th' wind-up, makin' sev'n. Sev'n majors! Tol'able gen'rous outfit fur one reg'ment, hain't it?"

Well, yes — I suppose it is; and yet all seven of our majors ably fill their positions, while Major Larry Callahan certainly fills *his* to the brim.

He never was enlisted, and his name has no place between the heavy leather covers of

the paymaster's cherished roll-book, and yet
he is just as much a part of the regiment as
the colonel commanding, or for that matter, as
the adjutant — and everybody knows how
big a man a gold-corded adjutant considers
himself. Why, I honestly believe that
Colonel Elliott — at such times as it seems
good to parade the Third, to exhibit the
power of the Commonwealth's " Strong Right
Arm "— never would think of giving the
order to start into motion his seven hundred
men unless he first had made sure that Larry
was at his post in front of the big bass-drum.
" Is Mulcahy in the ranks? " asked Hancock
at Gettysburg. " He is? Then let the
battle proceed ! " — and that rather well
illustrates our feelings in regard to our
seventh major.

It was two years ago last June when he
came to us. We just had topped off a week
of hard work in camp by a long, hot parade
through the dusty streets of the city, and six
of our twelve companies had been dismissed
to take trains for their out-of-town stations,
while the rest of the regiment, with the
drum-corps and the band, had marched up
town to the big armory. How he got by the

sentry at the door is more than I can tell, but somehow he managed it; I dare say he "sneaked it" in, under cover of the big drum which afterwards became his idol.

Captain Tom Stearns, of " A," had turned his company over to his first sergeant, and stood mopping his forehead with his handkerchief, as he watched his men slowly filing through the door of the drill-hall on their way upstairs to quarters, when he felt a tug at the skirts of his coat and heard a hoarse little voice demanding, " C'n I get a job carryin' de drum — say, can't I, mister ? I c'n tote it jus' 's well's dat coon youse got dere, an' I'd match d' rest o' de men better."

The captain looked down, and discovered, about at the level of his belt, a fiery red head, crowned by the ruin of a once-white straw hat; while a snub nose, an enormous mouth, a lavish display of freckles, and a twinkling pair of impish gray eyes made up the prominent features of the face upturned for his inspection.

"How in time did *you* get in here ? " politely asked Stearns, taking the intruder by the ear, and entirely ignoring his request.

"Follied de band, same's youse did. Le' go me ear, will yer! Say, c'n I carry de drum?"

"No, you can't. Now, 'bout face — and *march!*" replied the captain, releasing the boy's ear. "Look out for the guard at the door, or he'll make a pincushion of you when you go by him."

The ragged little urchin turned away, his face puckering into a mass of wrinkles in which a fair share of the freckles disappeared, dug a dirty fist into each eye, and started towards the door.

"Here, come back for a minute!" called Stearns, who, though dusty, hot, and tired, felt some compunction for his roughness, and in amends meditated the offering of a dime. "What are you crying about?"

"I ain't cryin'; an' I wanted de job — an' I'm hungry," said the boy, stopping and turning about.

"You *were* crying; and you can't have the job — and if you're hungry, why don't you go home to get a bite to eat, instead of hanging around processions?" said the captain, thrusting his hand into his pocket in search of a peace-offering.

" Ain't got no home t' go to," came the
brief but comprehensive reply.

" Haven't, eh ?   What's your name ? "

" Callahan — Larry Callahan," replied the
imp, coming a step nearer. " Say, *why* can't
I carry de drum? Dat coon's clo'es would
jus' about fit me, an' I sh'd t'ink de fellies
would ruther 'sociate wid me dan wid him."

This novel view of the fitness of things
seemed to come home with considerable
force to the tall captain, for he grinned and
said, " Well, I'm not sure that there isn't
something in that view of the situation.
Come along upstairs with me. I've got to
shift out of my uniform, and after that I'll
see what I can do for you. I'm hungry myself, and I've a faint suspicion that I'm also
thirsty, so I can sympathize with you to a
certain extent. Come along, ' Major ' — we'll
go foraging later."

In the company rooms there was tumult,
as there always is when sixty men find themselves jammed into a confined space and
simultaneously making the attempt to change
from the blue of the soldier to the plainer and
better-fitting costume of the civilian. Belt
buckles clattered, locker doors slammed, and

now and again a stray bar of the latest pop-
ular song brought forth either a rousing
chorus or else a roar of derision loud enough
to drown all other sounds. Conversation,
though rather fragmentary, was plentiful and
generously spiced, for the week in camp had
supplied the men with a brand-new stock
of gags and guys, and a torrent of chaff, in
which no one escaped, was raging unchecked.

" Who'll get the grand bounce for running
the guard last Thursday night?" roared a
voice, just as the captain and his new-found
acquaintance reached the door of the company quarters; and, " Smith—*Private* Smith!"
came back the answering yell.

" Yes, and the captain's got a recruit for
your place, me boy," said a man standing
near the door of the equipment-room, catching sight of Stearns' guest. " Come here,
Smithy, and get onto the new un that's going
to stuff out your uniform."

Stearns caught this last remark and smiled
at it, for he had found recent occasion to " read
the riot act " to one Private Smith, and he
remembered having said that he might feel
compelled to give that unruly warrior's uniform to some man more worthy of filling it.

In the snug officers' dressing-room the two lieutenants were engaged in freeing themselves from their heavy, uncomfortable dresscoats. Both looked up as the captain entered, and both laughed when he said, " Gentlemen, I have the honor of presenting Major Larry Callahan, who has inspected the regiment, and expresses complete satisfaction at its apparent efficiency. He more especially dwells upon the soldierly bearing of the drum-corps, though he criticises the complexion of the musician at the forward end of the boomer-drum, making the point that the presence of this black sheep among our tuneful lambs is in doubtful taste. I might add that he aspires to the position himself. Harry," to the second lieutenant, " you're smoking a cigarette! It's a nasty and often fatal habit — and you may give me one. It's the first article of war that a junior officer always must set 'em up for his superiors."

Stearns lighted the cigarette which this gentle hint brought forth from his subaltern's case, hung his heavy helmet upon a projecting gas-burner, and began leisurely to strip himself of his trappings.

" Where did you get it ? " asked the senior

lieutenant, nodding at Larry, and then turning to deposit his sword and belt in his
locker.

" He introduced himself to me, down in the
hall," replied the captain, sighing contentedly
as he flung his coat, with its row of jingling
marksman's medals, across the nearest chair.
" I'm to have the pleasure of his company at
lunch, as soon as I can get into street costume.
I crave food, and — by the Great White La-
bel ! — I crave pure, sparkling, cold water, or
anything cold and wet," and he softly hummed
to himself,

"No-bod-y knows how dry-I-am ! "

" Then you'll not come over to the club with
us ? " asked the younger lieutenant, ruefully.
" I know it seems a journey — way across
town on a day like this — but we'd counted
on your coming. Westbrook, of the Fourth,
is going to meet us, and possibly Van Sickles
will be there. Can't you fix it ? "

" No, not to-day, boys," said the captain,
taking from his locker a straw hat and plac-
ing it upon his head, with a mental compari-
son between its weight and that of his stiff,
spiked helmet; " I can't do it to-day.   I'm

going to the hotel for a bite, and then I'm bound straight for home — and a tub. Well, so-long! Remember, I must see you both here to-morrow afternoon — say, at half-past four. Come on, Major," and with a nod to his lieutenants he left the room.

The two younger men winked at each other, when the captain had disappeared, and the junior found occasion to remark, "Isn't he the gaudy old crank! Always picking up *some* curio or other — but this last 'find' of his comes near beating 'em all, eh?"

"It's one of his original ways of amusing himself," said the other, stepping to the mirror to adjust his tie, "and I dare say he enjoys it — but it isn't every one that could afford to go 'round in that way, with a dirty little ruffian tagging along at his heels. Come, Harry, aren't you ready yet? Well, get a gait on you, then — we don't want to keep Westbrook in agony any longer than necessary."

Over at the hotel, Stearns put his guest through a vigorous course of soap-and-towel exercise, and then ushered him into the gentlemen's *café*. To be sure, the waiters stared a bit when the tall captain and his dilapidated follower took possession of a table; but

Stearns was a frequent and liberal patron, and so — in spite of the exceedingly doubtful social standing of his companion — his order received prompt and willing attention. In the attack upon the food the honors were easy, but I'm reasonably sure that Larry gave good account of himself, for I've had the privilege of seeing him eat, in his company mess at camp, and so I'm able to vouch for his ability as a trencher-man.

So long as anything eatable remained on the table, conversation languished, but when the last crumb had disappeared — a matter to which Larry probably attended — the captain called for a glass of Kümel-and-ice, lighted a cigar, and said, " Well, Major Callahan, I trust that good digestion may be pleased to attend your appetite. How are you feeling — well lined ? "

" By Jinks ! " responded his guest, drawing his forefinger across his throat, " me tank's loaded 'way up t' here. Dat was dandy grub, de bes' I ever got."

" Can't you go something more ? " asked Stearns, much gratified at the spirit in which his hospitality had been received.

" No-o, I'm 'fraid I couldn't fin' de room,"

said the little fellow, slowly and with an air of deep regret. "I'd like t' 'commodate yer, but me 'commodations is all took up."

"If that's the case, then," said the captain, raising his glass to inspect the icy film with which its exterior had become coated, "we'll indulge in a gentlemanly chat. You're *sure* there's nothing else you want?"

"Well, I *smokes*," was Larry's suggestive response to this last question, "an' if youse 've got a cig'rette —"

"No, you *don't* smoke," put in the captain with some emphasis; "at least, you don't smoke here."

"Jus' 's yer say, o' course," replied his guest. "I don't care much 'bout it — on'y I t'ought p'r'aps 'twould be sort o' comp'ny t' yer."

"Well, it wouldn't be," said Stearns, pushing his chair a trifle farther away from the table. "And now, Major, suppose you tell me something about yourself. You say you've no home — what's the reason?"

The boy took a big gulp of water, hesitated for an instant, and then — catching the kindly expression in the captain's eye — rested his elbows upon the table, and told his

story: how he never had known a father;
how his mother had been sent away for a
long term at the women's reformatory; and
how he himself had been consigned to the
fostering care of an "Institution," but had
managed to evade the officer who had been
sent to conduct him to it.

"I s'pose I'd oughter ha' went t' de
'Home,'" admitted Larry, as he concluded his
brief and pitiful life's history; "but, hones', I
couldn't stan' it t' live de way dem kids does.
Dey gets dere t'ree meals a day, an' has a
place t' sleep — but dat's de whole of it.
An' as fer fun, why, what does *dey* know
'bout fun? Nothin'! Jus' youse look at 'em
sometime, an' see what a peepy-looking lot
dey is. Huh! dey ain't got no guts at all!"
and with this inelegant summing-up of the
moral effects of charity-rearing he dismissed
as absurd any possibility of his subjecting
himself to its tender mercies.

Captain Stearns heard the boy through, and
then for a few minutes sat thoughtfully
smoking. Finally he fixed his eyes upon the
little gamin, and abruptly asked, " Larry, are
you honest?"

" Yessir," replied the boy promptly, meet-

ing unfalteringly the captain's glance, "Yessir,
I'm dead on de square, an' if 'twasn't dat I'm
tryin' t' keep clear o' de 'Home,' I'd jus' 's
lives walk up t' any copper in town."

"That's business," said Stearns, "and I'm
glad to hear you say so. Now, I'm going to
give you some money, to keep you running
until tomorrow," — with this he drew out a
handful of change, — "and if you're playing
a square game with me you'll meet me to-
morrow noon, at the armory. Ask for Captain Stearns, and they'll let you in. I'm not
sure that I can do anything for you — I can't
today, at any rate — but we can talk over
the situation. Is it a go?"

"Yep, I'll be wid youse," said the boy,
hesitatingly taking the money which his en-
tertainer pushed across to him. "A quarter,
an' ten's t'irty-five — an' t'ree nick'ls is a
ha'f!" he went on, inspecting the tokens of
the captain's munificence. "Gee-cricketty!
w'at'll I do wid all de wealt'? Somebody'll
be marryin' me fer me forchune, 'f I ain't
careful!"

"You needn't spend it all, unless you have
to," said Stearns; "and if you have any of it
left, when you meet me tomorrow, I shall

think all the better of you. See here," he went on, yielding to a sudden whim, and tossing over a bill as he spoke, " suppose you put on a little style, and pay for this lunch of ours ! "

Larry's eyes twinkled as he clutched at the bill, and his mouth twisted itself into a grin of alarming proportions, but in an instant he assumed an air of unruffled composure, and beckoning to the waiter he inquired, " Sa-ay, cully, w'at's de taxes on dese 'freshments ? "

The astonished waiter, check in hand, for a moment stood glancing back and forth from the captain to the ragged but unabashed urchin. But Larry, waving the bill in his face, demanded, " Have youse b'en drinkin'? I axed youse de damage on de whole layout ! "

" Yas, sah," at length said the bewildered colored man, laying the check before the boy, " I heerd yo' ! "

" Den *dat's* all right," said Larry, picking up the check and glancing at it, only to break out with, " *W'at !* Two dollars an' a quarter? Why, I seen a place, on'y dis mornin', where dey gives youse a square meal — ' de bes' in de city,' it said on de sign — fer twenty cents ! "

" I think the check is correct," put in Stearns, smiling at the indignant expression on Larry's face and the disgusted look of the waiter. " Pay up — you're not being cheated."

After matters had been adjusted satisfactorily, the captain rose, held out his hand to his guest, and said, " Well, my boy, I must be going. Hope you enjoyed your lunch as well as I did mine. You'll drop in on me tomorrow, eh ? "

" Sure ! " replied the major, as he hunted for a pocket secure enough for the retaining of his suddenly acquired riches. " T'anks fer de grub, an' I'm 'bliged fer all dis mon'. An' *say*," coaxingly, " youse *must* have pull enough fer t' get me de place on de drum."

" I'm afraid I can't promise you that," said the captain, stopping as they reached the street, " for the drum-corps is rather outside my command. Well, I turn off here — good-bye, until tomorrow noon, Major."

The next forenoon Captain Tom varied his customary Sunday routine by taking a stroll through a quarter of the city with which he had but slight acquaintance, and casually dropping in at the station house of the precinct wherein Larry claimed former residence. A short chat with the lieutenant behind the rail brought out a number of unedifying facts about the lad's parentage, but Stearns found that his *protégé* had kept to the truth in telling his story; and so, considerably encouraged, he took a cab and went to meet his appointment at the armory.

Promptly at noon Major Larry reported with an elaborate sweep of the hand evidently meant to represent a military salute, and with a most expectant grin upon his mobile features.

"On time to a minute, that's proper," said Captain Tom, drawing out the sliding book-shelf of his desk, and utilizing it as a resting-place for his long legs. "Sit down, Larry, and we'll have a conference of the powers. How did your 'wealt'' hold out?"

Silently, but with a splendid air of pride, the boy drew a handful of coins from his pocket, came over to the captain's desk, and spread out his capital for inspection. Stearns counted the collection, and found that it aggregated eighty-two cents.

"H'm! so you're a young Napoleon of finance?" he said, as the little fellow put back the money into his pocket. "Well, tell me how you managed it."

"It was dis way," explained Larry, balancing himself on the back of a chair: "t' start wid, I had de ha'f youse gin me; an' den I went into de papey biz, and sol' enough t' make twenty cents more. Now, dat was 'velvet' — dem two dimes was — an' so I went t' pitchin' pennies wid de Pie Alley gang, an' I win t'irty more, makin' an even skimole. Well, I 'stood' on dat, 'cause I wasn't takin' no chances; an' I've got de stack, 'ceptin' t'ree cents I give Reddy Burns fer a shine, and fifteen w'at I blew in on me breakfus'. I slep' wid Reddy las' night, y' know, an' so I paid 'im fer me lodgin' by lettin' 'im black me boots — which wasn't no snap fer 'im, 'cause one o' dem boots is a cloth 'un, an' he kep' shinin' fer an hour 'fore he c'd get it t' glitterin'."

"Where did you get your supper?" inquired Stearns, leaning back in his chair and laughing at Larry's report, of his business transactions.

"Oh, I didn't want much supper, 'cause it was so late when you an' me was eatin'," returned the major, jingling his coins in his

pocket, "but I matched wid Slinky Smith **fer**
a piece o' pie, down in de alley, an stuck'm.
Say, I'll give back dat ha'f, if youse want it —
an' how 'bout de drum ?"

Well, Larry failed to get the position his
soul coveted — at least, at *that* time — but
when, after being in executive session for
more than an hour, the Conference of the
Powers adjourned, he had been appointed
" Company Kid " for " A " ; and on the
Monday night following he duly was introduced to the men, and was installed
formally in office.

From that day until now his popularity
steadily has grown greater — "and for good
cause." He has an inexhaustible fund of
Irish wit, by but one generation removed from
The Sod, and sharpened to the keenest edge
by the sort of life he has led. He is a tower
of strength in his command of modern Arabic,
that weird *patois* which reaches its full power
and beauty only in the streets of a great city.
He can sing, after a fashion, and his ability
to " do a dance act " is unquestioned, for
when he executes the steps it is with an air
of impressive earnestness and solemnity that
never fails to bring down the house. In fact,

since his advent, when we in the staff-room
hear a yell of delight come echoing down the
stairs and along the corridors, we grin sympa-
thetically one to another, and say, " Larry's
at it again — the little devil ! "

He is clever, too, at all sorts of things over
which the volunteer hates to fuss, and many
a dime comes his way in return for his skill
in polishing buttons and brasses for the lazy
men of the company — and " A," with fifty-
eight enlisted men upon its rolls, boasts of an
aggregate of fifty-seven who always are " in
fatigue," the remaining one being the tire-
less first-sergeant.

Yes, it was a great and ruby-lettered day
for " A " — the day when Larry came to it —
and in all its long history its quarters never
were kept so neat and clean, and its officers
and men never were entertained so well as
they have been since he began his genial
reign. And it was a great day for the regiment when our " seventh major " joined —
for Stearns' nickname of " Major " Callahan
has been adopted officially — because Larry's
fame has gone abroad in the land, and his
deeds have added new lustre to the name of
the Third.

Larry had been with us a little over a year when his great opportunity came to him. It was on a certain night when " A " had made arrangements for a smoke-talk, up in quarters — for Captain Stearns had met at his club one Lieutenant Hackett, of the regular cavalry, whom he had induced, after much patient persuasion, to come over to the armory and informally talk to the boys on the delights and discomforts of chasing Indians around through the Bad Lands.

Now, much as Larry respected his own corps, he held the regulars in even higher esteem, for he always had heard " The Army " held up as a pattern of all that is, in a military sense, good-and-holy and generally worthy of imitation by the hard-working and much-cursed-at volunteer. So when it came to his ears that a regular officer — and one, too, who actually had seen holes shot through people ! — really was going to honor his domain by his presence, he went to work with even greater energy than he had displayed at inspection time, and accomplished a house-cleaning such as would have warmed the heart of any New England matron to witness.

First he swept the floor, and then he dusted from the furniture the dust which had been raised by that operation, and then he swept up again the dust which the dusting had caused to return to the carpet — and then he paused, reflecting that, in the nature of things, he might continue this alternation forever unless he stopped. So, after a final dusting, he bent his energies to the arrangement of the chairs, marshalling them in ranks of military rigidity, and squinting critically along each row — muttering, " Back in de center, dere!" or "Up on de left, dad-gast-yer-shoulder-blades!" as he rectified the alignment. Then he polished the glasses of the pictures which form the nondescript art-gallery of the company; and finally he put the crowning touch to his afternoon's work by brushing the plush cushions of the great, carved chair in which the captain seats himself on occasions of state and ceremony.

He had been so busy that he had allowed his supper-hour to slip by unheeded, and when he happened to glance up at the clock he gave a low whistle of surprise, and said to himself, " Quarter pas' sev'n? *Wow!* how de time's be'n humpin' along? Well, I

s'pose I might's well skip me grub now: de
boys'll be showin' up in less 'n a shake."

He had given one last critical glance around
the room and was turning towards the door,
when his eye fell upon the great, wrought-
iron lamp which the company rifle-team had
won, a couple of years before, in a match
with " K," of the Fourth, and suddenly he
remembered that the oil in it nearly had been
burned out. Now, the boys of " A " regard
that lamp with particular affection, because
it was won in a contest to which they had
been egged-on by a series of peculiarly ex-
asperating events ; and it has become a time-
honored custom of the company to have the
lamp a-glow on every occasion when its
members are assembled by night. So Major Larry, knowing that the absence of its
cheerful rays would rouse the wrath of the
company kickers, picked up the heavy mass
of iron, and lugged it into the equipment-
room.

Here he filled the lamp, polished the chimney, trimmed the wick, lighted it, and had
raised his burden to carry it back to its
place — when, in some unexplained way, he
lost his grip upon it, and the whole heavy

affair went crashing down upon the floor.
In an instant the scattered oil was in a
blaze, and as Larry stood there, horrified at
his mishap, he saw the creeping tongues of
flame beginning to lick their way up the
varnished woodwork of the nearest lockers.
In two jumps he was at the door : a dozen
steps more brought him, yelling " Fire ! "
at the top-pitch of his voice, out into the
corridor — and then there came to him a
thought that almost stilled the beating of
his heart.

"Good Gawd ! " he gasped, stopping short
in his tracks, " dey's five hundred round o'
ca'tridge an' a ten-pound canister o' powder
in de nex' locker to de one dat's burnin' —
an' de door's locked ! Oh, what'll I do —
what'll I do ! "

Well, here's what he did do — and we have
fallen into the way of believing that no *man*
could have done much better work. On the
wall of the company room, in the midst of a collection of flint-lock muskets and other anti-
quated contrivances for achieving wild shots,
hung a heavy axe, a relic of the *ante-bellum*
days when "A" — at that time an inde-
pendent company — added dignity to its

parades by maintaining a small but ferocious-looking pioneer corps. Rushing in from the hallway, Larry tore this long-disused implement from its hooks, and dashed with it back into the equipment-room. By this time the flames had gained a fair start, and the blazing woodwork was crackling merrily, while the air was heavy and suffocating from the smoke of the burning oil and varnish.

With a single blow of the axe Larry sent the flimsy locker-door crashing from its hinges, and then, stooping down, he felt around for the powder can. *The locker was empty!*

"Yah! yer jay," he snarled at himself, as the smoke choked him; "yer poor, dam' jay — it's de *nex'* one!" and he snatched up the axe, swung it again, and splintered the burning door of the adjoining locker.

This time he hit his mark, for after an instant of frantic groping in the thick smoke, he got his hands upon the canister and flung it far from him, out into the room beyond. Then, by an effort almost superhuman, he dragged out the heavy, wooden case of cartridges, staggered with it through the flame and smoke — and fell in a dead faint across it, just as he cleared the threshold. And there, not five seconds later, the armorer found him, when he came rushing into the room with a line of stand-pipe hose, by the agency of which the blaze speedily was conquered.

Poor little major! His hands and face were cruelly burned, his thick crop of curly, red hair was wofully singed, and he had inhaled smoke enough to demoralize utterly his breathing-machinery. The firemen — for whom, upon hearing Larry's shout of alarm, the armorer had stopped to telephone — tenderly bore the lad downstairs to the staff-room; and just before the first of "A's" men strolled into the building an ambulance rolled away from the door, bearing the still unconscious form of the company kid.

Around the armory, that night, conversation was carried on in rather quiet tones, and nobody talked much except of Larry and his heroism. As soon as Stearns came in he was told of what had happened, and sending immediately for a cab he drove off post-haste to the hospital, leaving his lieutenants to receive his Army guest. In half an hour he was back again, with word that Larry, though badly burned and in great pain, was in no immediate danger — at which bit of news there came an audible sigh of relief from the men who had crowded around him. And then some one sung out " Hooray ! " and the rest came in with a shout that set the window panes to rattling.

Lieutenant Hackett was unfortunate in his audience that evening, for the boys — though they listened with studied politeness to his remarks — had something else upon their minds. But he got as much applause as any one could wish, when — at the close of his talk — he said, " Congress awards a Medal of Honor to those in the Army who perform deeds of exceptional bravery, and I can recall a long list of those who have received the decoration; but I wish to say that I can call to mind no instance of purer grit than that displayed today by your unlucky little comrade."

It certainly seemed a long time before Larry came back to us, but one night he turned up in our midst, as happy as ever and nine or ten degrees prouder than a colonel on the Governor's staff — for Stearns had fitted him out with a complete drum-corps uniform, made

expressly for him, and Colonel Elliott had used
his influence to make for his especial benefit
a vacancy at the advance-end of the big
drum. The affairs of the regiment ran more
smoothly after his return, and I can remember
the change in the aspect of "A's" men — for
Larry was himself again, and funnier than
ever.

But there was still more glory awaiting him.
About two weeks after he had " re-joined," we
had a battalion-drill in the big hall, and after
it a dress parade. The companies had got
wind of what was coming, and the ranks were
full. It was Larry's first appearance with
the drum-corps, and when the field music
"sounded-off" along the line, the air with
which he stepped out lacked little of being
superb.

The adjutant had received the reports and
published the orders, when the colonel, in a
low tone, said a word or two to him which
caused him to face about and walk along the
front of the battalion to the spot where Larry
was standing, stiff as a post, among the musi-
cians. In a moment he returned, bringing
the bewildered lad with him, and then the
colonel stepped a pace forward to meet him,

and pinned upon his breast a bronze Maltese
cross, inscribed:

"A" Co., 3rd Infantry
TO
𝕵𝖆𝖗𝖗𝖞 𝕮𝖆𝖑𝖑𝖆𝖍𝖆𝖓
FOR
DISTINGUISHED BRAVERY.

And beside this simple decoration he fastened
the regimental badge, brilliant with its glittering gold and bright enamel — a tribute
from the officers of the field and staff.

Of course the colonel made a little speech,
but it was a short one and the words were
simple. As he finished he shook hands with
the boy, and then brought the battalion to a
" carry," after which he called out, " Present :
arms ! "

Up with a snap came the long line of rifles;
down drooped the colors until their golden
fringes touched the floor; the flashing blades
of the officers rose and fell — and little Larry
Callahan had been saluted by the crack regiment of the Old Commonwealth!

" Now, adjutant," said Colonel Elliott, when
the line again stood at attention, " just take
Major Larry to the left of the line and march

him along the front to the right, so that all the
men can see him. Chin in, Larry, my boy —
and keep a stiff upper lip!"

The boy said never a word, but saluted and
then started off with the adjutant. For a time
discipline went into eclipse: the men yelled
" *Hi! Hi!* " and thumped their rifle-butts
upon the floor, until the great hall shook to
its very foundations — while the officers not
only neglected to check the uproar, but even
went so far as to help in swelling it.

Larry stood it all like a Spartan, tramping
along with eyes to the front and head well up,
until he came abreast of the center, where "A"
stood in line, with the colors. But here he
broke down, hid his face behind the adjutant's
arm, and sobbed as though his heart would
burst, when the sixty men — his friends and
comrades, every one of them — broke into
a wild yell of applause as he came before
them.

Well, that ended the ovation; for Captain
Stearns, seeing at a glance that the strain had
been too heavy for the boy to bear, raised his
hand in a warning gesture to his men, picked
up the little hero, swung him up upon his
shoulder, and marched with him straight

along the line and then out of the hall, leaving his company to take care of itself as best it might. And yet, so far as my knowledge goes, Colonel Elliott never has taken the slightest notice of this most un-military proceeding of the captain's!

CONCERNING

THE

VALUE OF SLEEP

CONCERNING

THE

VALUE OF SLEEP.

OVER the mantel in Major Pollard's smoking-room, in a heavy, elaborately carved frame, there hangs a colored photogravure of De Neuville's " *Une Pièce en Danger*," that terrible group — outlined against a gray background of battle-haze — of rearing, plunging horses, and of fiercely fighting German cavalrymen and French gunners, surging in desperate struggle around a limbered gun. Many a time I've sat and looked up at it, idly wondering whether the troop of Cuirassiers, dimly visible in the drifting smoke at the right, would come rushing into the rumpus in time to save the battered handful of artillerymen and the piece to which they so grimly and absurdly

cling.   But all this is neither here nor there:
for the picture tells its own story — while
the story I have in mind to tell is quite
another one.

It's not a very thrilling story.   In fact, I
doubt if it will have much interest for any
one outside the regiment; but it will please
Pollard to see it in cold, black type, and
I'm indebted to him for so many comfortable
hours, passed in the fragrant atmosphere of
that same smoking-room of his, that I gladly
take this opportunity to even up in the matter of obligations.

It so happens that these are times of peace,
and — though there are a few of us who
childishly consider that the very peacefulness
of the times affords a most excellent opportunity to prepare for war — the tranquillity
of everything bids fair to continue undis-
turbed.   But even in quiet days something
in the blood of the Anglo-Saxon craves
rivalry and contention, and so from year to
year we of the volunteers get together and
shoot — projecting much lead at remote bulls-
eyes, in order to find out who are the most
disgracefully erratic marksmen.

Now, in these days the soldier who cannot

shoot — however pleasing to the eye he may be — is of no earthly sort of use. Pollard can shoot. On battalion drill he sometimes may find himself at a loss for just the proper command ; and once, in earlier days, I heard him direct his astonished company to execute " Right forward, fours *left !* " — but there is no denying that he can shoot.

To the scroll-work on the bottom of the great carved frame enclosing the picture of which I have spoken, there is fastened a bevelled, gilded panel, very modestly lettered in black, " LAST SHOT, 1890 : " and this ideally simple inscription commemorates a shot which — if not " heard 'round the world " — has not yet ceased to be ·remembered whenever, in the company-rooms of the Third, men drift into rifle-talk.

Pollard was not always a major. It was only last October, when, in the nature of things, leaves were falling freely, that two pairs of bright, golden ones found a resting-place upon his broad shoulders. Back in '90, he was captain of " M " Company ; and one night, early in September of that year, he found himself badly out of sorts at the news that one of the best men on his company rifle-team had slipped, fallen, and gone into temporary retirement with a broken wrist.

"It's too blistering bad!" said Pollard, as, late that night, he stood upon the steps of the armory and scowled out into the darkness. "Even with Harvey on the team, we had no sure thing — 'H' is shooting so like sin! — but now I don't know *where* we are. Well, Johnny, you'll have to do your cleverest, and perhaps we'll get there in spite of you."

"Thanks!" said the younger officer, thus addressed. "You're mighty encouraging, aren't you? Well, I've always said that I ought to have been put on the team, and to-morrow I'll prove it. Wow! how it blows!"

"Yes, it's breezy," assented Pollard, listening to the lively rat-a-tat played by the loose flag-halliards upon the tower-staff, "and later it'll rain. To-morrow, though, will be a good enough day; see if it isn't. Come along, my son, it's high time we were getting bedward."

"Now, see here, Johnny," he observed, a moment later, stopping at the head of the

street, " I've got to make good time to catch
my train, but I'll pause to remark that you
must go home *now !* Don't color any pipes
to-night; don't take a pencil and go to
figuring on the scores, for matches aren't
won in that way; and go to sleep early.
Sleep is the all-important thing, and without
it you'll not do anything to-morrow. Got
all that? Good-night," and, tossing to his
shoulder the rifle he carried, he rapidly
strode away.

" Humph! he thinks I can't hold up my
end," thought the lieutenant, glancing at the
receding figure of his superior officer ; " I'll
show him! I'm sorry for Harvey, but I'm
inclined to think that his place will be
filled tolerably well. Pollard's right, though,
about the sleep question. I'd like to play
a game or two of billiards, but," heroically,
" but — I'll go home."

Meanwhile Pollard was hastening towards
his train. As he came in sight of the
illuminated clock-dial upon the station his
rapid walk quickened into a trot ; and the
trot, in its turn, gave place to a run when,
as he passed in through the wide doorway,
he heard the clang of the last gong. How-

ever, by a spirited dash down the long
platform, he caught the handrail of the
last car in the moving train, and swung
himself, panting but triumphant, upon the
steps.

"Enemy behind us?" inquired the brake-
man, pausing in his task of knotting the
dangling bell-cord, and glancing down at the
uniformed figure below him.

"Didn't have time to see," said Pollard,
laughing at the aptness of the question. "I
ran without waiting to find out," and, as
the train swung around a curve and rattled
over a switch, he lurched through the doorway, and dropped into the nearest empty
seat. Fifteen minutes later he found himself at his destination, and leaving behind
him the oasis of brightness formed by the
lights of the little station he plunged into
the desert of suburban gloom lying beyond.

It certainly was not a cheerful night to be
abroad. The sky was black as a hat, and
the wind swept by in gusts that threatened
to extinguish the street lamps which, at rare
intervals, twinkled along the lonely way. It
was early in September, and many of the
houses still were closed; while the lateness of

the hour made those that were occupied seem dark and untenanted.

Half unconsciously Pollard began to whistle " The White Cockade," and his step fell as naturally into the cadence of the air as if he were following the regimental drum-corps. A short walk brought him to his own house, — standing shadowy and silent among the surrounding trees, — and, dropping upon the floor of the porch the butt of his rifle, he fumbled in his pocket for his keys. He threw open the door, stepped into the yawning blackness of the unlighted hall, and groped his way along the wall to the electric button which should light the chandelier. He pressed it, but no blaze of light followed the sharp click. Once more he touched the button, and then, when again the light failed to respond, cautiously felt his way along the floor until he stood beneath the chandelier, and, reaching up his hand, found that the gas was turned off.

" Hello ! " he said to himself. " That's funny — altogether *too* funny ! I certainly left the gas turned on, ready for the spark," and instinctively he fell back a pace, and then stepped out upon the porch.

"*Did* I leave the burner like that?" he queried, as he stood peering into the dense shadow before him. "Blessed if I can remember! Somehow, though, it seems queer," and, unbuttoning his military great-coat, he slipped his hand beneath its lapel and drew a cartridge from the canvas belt which hung from his shoulder diagonally down across his chest.

"I'm not sure that this is a very sandy proceeding," he thought, pushing home the cartridge, and with a vicious snap locking behind it the breech-block of his rifle; "but if anybody's in the house I'm going to have an even show with him."

Balancing his piece in his left hand, he again entered the hall, turned on the gas, touched the button, and when the jet of flame flared up, glanced quickly into the empty rooms on either side. All was as he had left it in the morning; and after intently listening for a moment he closed and bolted the hall door, and went upstairs to his own rooms.

Once in the room he called his Den, he took off his great-coat, drew the cartridge from his rifle, and returned it to its place in the long row of leaden-tipped, shiuing copper cylinders in his ammunition-belt, and tossed the belt upon the lounge. Then he went over to the mantel, picked out from the litter upon it a short, dark briarwood, and proceeded to comfort himself with smoke.

"Humph! that was a pretty weak exhibition," he grunted, stooping over to unlace his shoes. "Come to think of it, when I went out this morning I found that I'd left the light burning all night, and — I remember it now clearly enough — turned off the gas to save the bother of going over to punch the button."

He tossed aside his shoes, put on a pair of easy slippers, and lighted a candle. "May as well see that all's tight," he soliloquized, starting on a tour of the silent house; "here goes for 'grand rounds'! It *is* lonesome, with the family across the water. Wish they'd come home! Can't say I blame the servants for packing up and leaving; but mother'll be wild when she gets my letter telling that they've gone."

From room to room, trying the fastenings of doors and windows, he went his rounds. All was secure; so, pausing on his way to touch the button extinguishing the hall light, he slowly climbed the stairs again, locked the door of his Den, and with a yawn flung himself into his easy-chair.

For a few minutes he quietly sat thinking; then, taking from his pocket a pencil, he began to jot down upon the back of an old envelope a series of figures — his estimate of the scores likely to be made in the match of the morrow.

" Perhaps we can pull it out," he muttered, eying the columns of figures upon the crumpled bit of paper; "*perhaps* we can; but it'll be cruelly close! 'H' is good for almost anything up to five points over centres, and — unless I can get more than I think I can out of Johnny — we're not liable to run much above that. Confound Harvey! Why couldn't he pick out a more convenient time for breaking himself?"

Here Pollard guiltily started, sprang to his feet, and hastily began to throw off his garments, for the clock in the hall outside had begun to sound off the first of the twelve slow strokes of midnight. "I'm better at preaching than at practising," he thought, grinning at the remembrance of his parting injunctions to his junior; "I've broken two-thirds of the rules I laid down for Johnny. Well, I'm an old hand at this business, and even if I've wasted a half-hour or so I shall get enough sleep to put me into shape," with which consoling reflection he took a long, parting pull at his pipe, shook the ashes from it, put out the light in the Den, and went into his bedroom adjoining.

Taking a revolver from the drawer of the bureau, he tucked it under his pillow; and after locking the door, leading from the chamber into the hall, kicked his slippers across the room, finished his disrobing, and tumbled into bed. "There it comes!" he drowsily murmured, as a stronger gust of wind was followed by a few scattering drops, and then by a driving dash of rain. "Well, it'll rain itself out before morning; to-morrow's *got* to be a good day. H'm! it's pretty quiet out here! I'm sick and tired of this suburban business; think I'll have to set up bachelor-rooms in town, after the family gets back." And with this resolve — which he later carried into effect — he fell asleep, with the fingers of one hand lightly and comfortably resting upon the butt of his pistol.

For more than an hour the rain fell heavily; then, as suddenly as it had begun, it ceased. With it the wind died away, leaving a silence so intense that when the hall clock gave out two resonant strokes the sound echoed and reëchoed through the house. Ten minutes later the deep quiet was broken by a sharp crack, as of splintering wood, and then, for a time, all again was still.

Now, Pollard sleeps lightly, and the unusual sound, insignificant though it was, started him up upon his elbow, with eyes wide open and ears strained to catch the slightest creak or jar. Three minutes passed. He was about to relax his motionless position of listening, when there came to his ear a muffled noise that made him slip cautiously, revolver in hand, from bed.

"Shoving up a sash, by thunder!" he said to himself. "It's lucky that I came out, instead of going to a hotel as I thought of doing. Let's see what's going on."

He crept to the door, pressed his ear to the thin panel, and listened; but after a few seconds he straightened up, and disgustedly addressed himself thus: "See here, Pollard — *Captain* Pollard! — what sort of soldier are you? Your heart's thumping so that you can't hear anything else, and your knees are about as near wobbling as they well can be without doing it! I know you're not afraid — but what *is* the matter with you?" Again he put his ear to the door, and this time distinctly heard from below sounds which plainly indicated that some one was at work in the dining-room.

"Now, I'd give something," thought the silent listener at the door, "to know just how my side of this campaign ought to be conducted. In the first place, I'd be a heap sight more courageous if I had on my trousers and shoes. I'm no Highlander; I'm just an ordinary citizen-soldier — and if I've got to go into action I'd much prefer to form for the attack in less light-marching-order than this. But if I leave the door — confound it all! — I'll lose touch with the enemy. I want my clothes, but I *must* know what's being done down there."

Still keeping to his post at the door he noiselessly cocked and uncocked his weapon, in order to make sure that the cylinder freely revolved. Below, for a moment, all was quiet; then came a sound which Pollard interpreted to be the metallic clink of hastily gathered silverware. "That'll keep 'em busy for a moment," he thought, leaving the door, "and I'll have time to put on my armor. There isn't much stuff in the sideboard — only a few spoons and forks. Lucky that we sent the bulk of the silver in to the vaults! Here are my trousers — and here's one slipper — where in glory's the mate to it? Oh, if I only find it I'll make a vow to put my foot-gear, after this, under my pillow every night!" For an instant longer he cautiously pawed around in the darkness, but the missing slipper refused to be found, and so, half-shod, he crept back to the door to resume his listening.

The startled feeling that had come upon him when so suddenly awakened had gone, and he was perfectly cool and determined. "Well, what's the next move?" he asked himself, as he stood listening to the faint sounds below. "So long as I stay here I'm safe enough, but it seems a trifle white-feathery to let 'em have full swing down there, without lifting a finger to spoil their sport. Of course I can scare 'em out of the house easily enough — a couple of thumps on the floor would do it — but I want a *shot* for my money. What sort of good were old Bones' 'Emergency Lectures'? I went to 'em all, last winter, and yet here's an emergency — and I don't know exactly what to do with it!"

For a time there had been a cessation in the noises below stairs, but suddenly Pollard became aware of stealthy footfalls, and then the stairs lightly creaked under an ascending tread.

"They're coming up!" he said to himself; "more than one of 'em, too — I can tell by the sound! Well, this campaign's planned itself out now. I'm going to fight on inside lines," and gently disengaging his slippered foot from its encumbrance, he stole barefooted into the outer room, and took his station at the door.

"Now, this is going to be almost *too* easy; and all because the inspired architect who planned this house saw fit to locate a push-button in the wall, just outside!" thought Pollard, as there came to his ear a subdued whispering which indicated that the intruders had reached the head of the stairs, and had paused for a short consultation. "I'll just try a pot-shot at these gentlemen from inside

here; and then — when they break for downstairs — step out, touch up the light in the
lower hall, and halt 'em where they stand."

Softly falling back a couple of paces, he
pointed his pistol towards the door, and fired.
In the confined air of the closed room the
report was deafening, and Pollard's ears rang
merrily, when — taking it for granted that his
visitors must be in full retreat — he sprang
to open the door and put into execution the
remaining part of his plan of operations.
In clumsy haste he groped in the darkness
for the key; but at that instant a shot rang
out in the hall, and a bullet tore its way
through the panel of the door and embedded
itself in the opposite wall, making a most
unexpected interruption in the programme
that he had laid out for himself to follow.

" Stay where y' are — *d' yer hear?* — stay
where y' are," commanded a hoarse voice from
without, "while we're gettin' clear, or I'll
blow yer blasted head off, yer — " here came
a burst of abusive profanity that sent Pollard's
blood to the boiling-point.

" All right; but get out lively!" said he,
still keeping his hand upon the key, but
swinging to one side in order to be out of

direct range of the frail door. At the words, a second bullet came splintering through the wood, as if to give emphasis to the remarks which so had annoyed him, and then there followed a noisy rush of feet down the stairs.

Without an instant's hesitation Pollard wrenched open the door, jumped into the hall, and calling, " Up with your hands ! " set ablaze the gas in the chandelier below. Midway of the stairs, as he stood in the shadow of the upper landing, he saw the two marauders, who had been checked in their flight by the unexpected burst of light.

" Come — *up with those hands!* " said Pollard sternly, levelling his weapon, " or I'll blow *your* blasted — " but the sentence was left incomplete, for with cat-like swiftness one of the men turned and fired at him. But Pollard, heavily built though he is, can be quickness itself when occasion demands, and at the flash of the other's revolver his own weapon spoke sharply, sending a cruel bit of lead ploughing its way through flesh and sinew and bone. With a gasp of pain the man at whom he had fired reeled over against the balusters, and, as his shattered arm fell helplessly at his side, his smoking pistol dropped from his grasp and went clattering down the stairway.

"Have you got enough?" said Pollard, swinging over his weapon, and covering the unwounded burglar. "There's more of the same sort where that came from — if you want it!"

"*Don't shoot again!*" said the second man, throwing up his hands. "We give in!"

"'Thereby showing more sense than you've shown yet," returned the barefooted master of the situation, coming forward a few steps. "Now, listen to me. Take your pal down to that big leather chair in the corner of the hall — and don't make any fatal mistake by trying to pick up that gun on the stairs!"

"And now," he went on, following the doleful procession downstairs, "get his coat off, and see how badly he's hit. Bone's broken, eh? H'm! that's pretty bad! Well, get to work to stop the bleeding; I'll tell you how," and under his directions the wounded arm was bandaged up in a rough, though effective fashion.

"And what'll I do with you *now?*" said Pollard reflectively, as he stood looking at the two crestfallen intruders. " What's that? ' I shot first ! ' Well, that's so ; but I also shot last — and best. It's no use ; I've got to turn you over, much as I dislike to do it."

Here there came heavy footsteps upon the porch outside, followed by a sharp pull at the door-bell, and Pollard, keeping one eye upon his two bad men, edged to the door and opened it.

" Come in," he said politely, as he caught the glitter of a policeman's buttons ; " come in ; but don't feel obliged to club me. In fact, you needn't club anybody ; the row's all over, and we're all friends here."

" I'd have been here sooner," said the panting patrolman, reaching into his pocket for his handcuffs, " only when I heard the shooting I ran to the box, and rang in the wagon-call. The team'll be along in a min- ute. Well, you've done a good job here, sir, and I guess you didn't need much help about it, judging by the looks of things."

" No, I suppose I didn't," admitted Pollard, shivering slightly as the damp air of the early morning found its way through the thin, white garment which modestly draped

the upper portion of his person; " I daresay
I didn't; but ten minutes ago, all the same,
I wouldn't have refused a small amount of
assistance   Br-r-r! Chilly, isn't it? If you'll
stay here and entertain my guests for me,
I'll run upstairs for a minute and throw on
some more cloth."

Stooping to pick up the burglar's revolver,
which still lay where it had fallen upon the
stairs, he ran up to his room, struck a light,
and without bothering over the matter of
hosiery, slipped on his shoes.   Then he strug-
gled into his warm, military coat, lighted a
cigar, and descended to the hall, just in time
to hear the rapid beat of hoofs and the
crunching sound of wheels that told of the
patrol-wagon's approach.

In a few minutes more all was over; Pollard had told his story to the officers and the
few excited neighbors who had ventured out
to investigate the cause of the tumult, and the
wagon had rumbled away with its two un-
willing passengers and their guards.

" Well, that's over with and out of the
way," said Pollard to himself, after he had
made secure the window through which, by
forcing off the catch, the burglars had gained

entrance; "out of the way for the present, at least: to-morrow, I suppose, I'll have to go through all manner of fuss at the station — and later I'll be summoned to court to help jug those poor devils for ten years or so apiece. Confound 'em! why couldn't they have gone to some house where the people were away, instead of stirring *me* up?"

He yawned, and slowly made his way up to his Den, pausing for a minute to inspect the perforated panels of the door. Of the three holes in the woodwork, two were clean-cut and smooth, showing that the lead had gone through from without; the third, ragged and surrounded by splinters, told of the shot that he had fired.

"I'll have to get that door patched up before mother comes home," he reflected, as he passed into the room, "or she'll have a most awful attack of nerves when she sees it. Hello! it's well along towards three o'clock, and — Great Jupiter's thunderbolts! I'd forgotten about that match!"

He dropped into a chair, and stared blankly at the carpet. How on earth could he manage to be in two places at once? He had promised to report in the morning at the police-station, and yet he *must* leave town on an early train with his company team!

"Phew! I *am* let in for it!" he thought. "Here's another 'emergency' not provided against in Bones' lectures. I've ordered the team to report to me at eight o'clock, and if I go over to see the police I can't get to the armory in time. On the other hand, if I fail to show up at the station I'll more than likely succeed in mixing myself up in some unholy legal mess. Now, *how* can I surround the situation?"

It certainly was a perplexing problem: but Pollard is not of those who are prodigal of time in the making up of their minds, and his decision was reached in short order.

"I don't know much about law," said he to himself, as for the second time that night he pulled off his shoes; "but, for the present, the police will have to go to Halifax! Perhaps I'm showing contempt of court, or something else of the sort that will get me into calamity. I can't help it if I am! I'm going out with the team, even if I land in jail for doing it. Lord! I'm in fine, fat form for shooting! To-morrow'll find me — *to-day'll* find me, I mean — as nervous as a Salem witch," and groaning dismally at his hard luck, he hunted up an alarm-clock, set it for an early hour, and prepared to snatch what little sleep he yet might be able to get.

With a vivid recollection of recent experiences he carefully assembled his slippers at the foot of the bed, and then crawled beween the sheets. "I must'nt let the boys know anything about this," he reflected, as he lay waiting for sleep to come to him; "it would break 'em up. Let me see, the morning papers go to press somewhere about two o'clock, so the story can't leak out in that way. Well, it's tolerably certain that *I'm* out of the race. It would take a wooden man to go through a night like this without getting the quivers. I'll be satisfied if I can put my ten shots anywhere on the target."

Rolling over upon his side he closed his eyes, murmuring, "Glad I winged that fellow, after all; he did his best to lay me out, and his remarks were extremely ungentlemanly. Take it all together, it was a pretty lively fray while it lasted. Can't say I'd care to go through another like it — not just yet, anyway."

After an hour of turning and tossing, Pollard succeeded in dropping into a troubled sort of doze ; but, as it seemed to him, he hardly had lost consciousness when the merciless little bell of the alarm-clock began to rattle out its diabolical reveille, compelling him, heavy-eyed and in a most villainous frame of mind, to struggle out from beneath the tangled bedclothes.   A plunge into a tub of cold water did something towards freshening him up a bit, but when he buckled on his ammunition-belt and picked up his rifle he swore softly to himself at the day's prospect.   However, a quick walk in the crisp air of the September morning sent the blood jumping cheerfully through his veins; and after he had made, at an in-town hotel, a halt long enough for the total destruction of a thick and generous tenderloin of steak, he strode over to the armory in a more confident mood.

And the match?   Well, it was much like a hundred other matches that have been shot over the same stretch of level, close-cropped greensward : but "II" shot like sin, and it *was* a cruelly close thing — as Pollard had thought it would be — from the time when the first bullet was sent singing on its way towards the distant targets, until the last disk had been pushed up from the marking-pit.

According to his custom, Pollard coached his team until, except himself, all had fired; then, with a coolness at which he found himself wondering, he took his place at the firing-point and prepared to shoot his own score. Shot by shot the sergeant at the blackboard chalked up the results : three centres; a bullseye; another lone centre; two more bullets in the black ; a fifth centre ; a fourth bullseye — and one shot yet to be fired !

With his eyes upon the target, Pollard was slipping a cartridge into the chamber when he felt a touch upon his sleeve, and turning, saw Lieutenant Johnny, flushed with excitement, standing beside him. " Polly," whispered the youth, with utter forgetfulness of rank and title, " Polly, ' II ' has finished ! I'd never think of doing this with anybody besides you — but, to win, you'll have to get a ' bull.' A ' four ' isn't going to do the trick, for we'd be outranked on a tie. *You've got to land in the black !* "

"Yes?" said the captain, dryly. " Well, Johnny, fall back — the gun might explode, you know," and with a last glance at the drooping wind-flags, he stiffened himself into position, gently lined the sights upon the far-off speck of black, and fired.

For five breathless seconds, while the little puff of pungent smoke lazily floated away, there was silence; and then, when the white disk went slowly creeping up over the face of the target to find its resting-place upon the bull's eye, there came from the watching men of "M" a sharp gasp of relief, followed by an exultant yell of victory.

"*Steady!*" commanded Pollard, swinging around upon his heel. "What's the matter with you, boys? Do you want to make people think we've never won before?" and, bending over to pick up his lightened cartridge belt, he walked towards the tents.

Late that afternoon, as the members of Pollard's team sat together in the smoker, on their way back to town, a newsboy entered the car. Pollard beckoned him to his side, bought an afternoon paper, and after rapidly running his eye down the columns of the outer page, handed the sheet to his lieutenant.

"Holy Smoke!" said that young man, catching a glimpse of the bold type heading the story of his captain's night adventure, "Is *that* the way you slept last night? Well, I'll be —"

"You'll be asked to 'send in your papers,' Johnny," interrupted Pollard, with an awful yawn, "if you ever again speak to me when I'm at the firing-point in a match. You came pretty close to queering my score for me, this afternoon. Yes, that's the way I slept last night, and I think I'm beginning to feel it a trifle," whereat he again yawned, and then settled himself more comfortably upon the dusty cushions of the seat.

Well, that's all there is to the story. About the picture in Pollard's smoking-room? Oh, the men of his team gave that to him, thinking that he would like to have something by which to remember the cleverest shot he ever fired. Over in the big armory, in the company-room of " M," there hangs another picture, just like that one — the trophy awarded by the Commonwealth to the team winning the championship of the regiment.

www.ingramcontent.com/pod-product-compliance
Lightning Source LLC
Chambersburg PA
CBHW030123030726
47498CB00007B/2529